Death of a Lov

He fixed his eye ⋯⋯⋯⋯⋯⋯⋯⋯⋯ w
ball. It would be a ⋯⋯⋯⋯⋯⋯⋯ t-
ily and followed t⋯⋯⋯⋯⋯⋯⋯ g
back slowly, his left shoulder moving gradually to a
point a few inches from his long chin. The diamond
on the bright ball winked at him. He reached the top
of his backswing.

Someone screamed.

Root swung wildly through the ball, catching it on
the toe of the club and sending it whistling off high
and right, where it was caught by a gust of wind and
whipped away from the fairway to finish in the
deepest patch of rough on the course.

Root began a curse and glared at the spinney
where the noise had come from.

Lecky looked concerned.

"Bad luck," he offered pacifically.

"Did he have to yell just then!"

"I watched it all the way. Bad luck. You might find
it," said Lecky.

Root knew it was a lost ball, but he managed a
wry smile.

"Aye," he agreed. "But I'll play a provisional just
in case."

Root was about to place the new ball on the tee
when another sound came from the spinney. It was
as impatient and full of emotion as the high-pitched
scream which had spoiled his drive. But this one
made him freeze on the backswing.

"Murder!"

Other titles in the Walker British Mystery Series

BRIAN
BALL

Death of a Low-Handicap Man

WALKER AND COMPANY · NEW YORK

First published in the United States of America
in 1978 by the Walker Publishing Company, Inc.

This paperback edition first published in 1984.

ISBN: 0-8027-3063-9

Library of Congress Catalog Card Number: 78-60749

Printed in the United States of America

10 9 8 7 6 5 4 3 2 1

For
Margaret and Mac
Peter and Marion
Andy and Gwen
and, of course, Reg and Pat

Acknowledgement

The author wishes to acknowledge the courtesy of the Royal and Ancient Golf Club of St Andrews in permitting the use of quotations from the *Rules of Golf*.

Death of a Low-Handicap Man

One

'The Game of Golf consists in playing a ball from the teeing ground
into the hole . . .'

It always pleased Root to see another golfer weighing up the first at
Wolvers. He watched Jack Lecky's face. It showed delight; and then
puzzlement. The long, broad swathe of grass, newly-cut and
downhill to the harlequin-patterned green, would help any drive on
its way. But there was something wrong with the perspective: and
Lecky saw it. The green with its bunkers at each side was further
away than it seemed. Root found himself grinning. Jack Lecky had
taken in the significance of the depression about a hundred and fifty
yards down the fairway.

    'Not what it seems, Arthur?'

    'No Jack.'

    'Longer than it looks, too. A nice hole.'

    'Aye, nice.'

    Rabbits and tigers alike, men who played twice a year and those

1

only deep snow kept off the course; Bentley owners and me who could barely raise the annual subscription : all agreed on one thing. Wolvers, with its castellated and mock-crenellated mansion set in rolling parkland, was the finest course in industrial Yorkshire. And the first hole was the best.

'We should get some distance,' said Lecky.

'Aye.'

It had been a dry summer, weather which brought yelps of joy to the 24-handicap men who muffed and squeezed and topped their drives but finished a clear hundred and thirty yards from the tee no matter how erratically they swiped at the ball.

'Can we drive now, Arthur ?' Lecky asked.

'Not yet. If you crack one properly, it could catch old Cathcart.' He pointed to four players making their way to the green. 'It'll be a slow job. One week it took them nearly five hours to do the Medal round. The four after them came back raving.' Lecky was still starting at the dip, so Root went on. 'One of them said he wouldn't have Cathcart cutting grass, let alone golfing. That'd be Tom. Yes, Tom Tyzack. He swore he'd report Cathcart for slow play.'

A light rain began, but it was not enough for either man to get out the waterproofs.

Root noted with satisfaction that Cathcart was squaring up for his third shot. The knowing old boys generally played short at the first. It was all of four hundred and twenty yards from tee to flag and their drives, though straight, weren't long. So Cathcart and his slow, old crew would plonk one down the middle, take a six or a five iron to somewhere within range, and chip on up to the pin. They would always be down in five, often in four, whilst stronger and younger men took massive swipes and higher scores.

'You take the honour, Jack,' he said to Lecky, but Jack Lecky wasn't listening. He had noticed the stewardess.

She was trotting across from the early nineteenth-century mansion that was now the clubhouse to the bright blue tent with a tray of glasses. She wobbled on high heels in a way that every right-thinking man at Wolvers found highly agreeable. She stopped to talk to a younger woman. Root would have waved, but Margaret Hughes

2

hadn't seen him.

'That's our Elaine,' said Root. 'The toast of the club.'

'She's a big girl.'

Root grinned at his new neighbour. Lecky was getting over the loss of his wife. Not that she'd been much of a loss from what his wife had learned. It hadn't been much of a marriage – twelve years of it, and she didn't want kids. And when Lecky moved to South Yorkshire she wouldn't join him.

'You can chance your luck there, if you like,' he said. 'You won't be the first.'

Lecky's eyes danced.

'She *is* a big girl.'

The stewardess wore the black lacy dress of her kind. She was a pretty, well-preserved woman of thirty-two or three, and she knew that her Sunday morning crossing from the mansion to the refreshment tent was an event in the lives of the members of Wolvers. She allowed her natural abundance of flesh to manifest itself.

'Wait till you're a member,' Root advised. 'The Committee wouldn't like it if you tried it on now.'

'They wouldn't?'

'No.'

'I'll remember.'

Over Lecky's features came that odd look of abstraction and intentness that every dedicated golfer shows when he is preparing to drive. Lecky waggled his hips in the approved manner; he broke his wrists as he tried a preliminary half-swing; he pointed his left shoulder down the middle.

His concentration was disturbed by a ringing giggle from below the spinney, however. The pro would have his brown hands on some young woman as he explained the overlapping grip. So Lecky had to go through the whole performance once more.

When he did hit the ball, it was with a slow, easy swing which smacked it cleanly in the middle of the club two hundred and fifty yards down the fairway. It bored through the wind, barely deviating in flight. Then it pitched beyond the hidden dip, straight into the emerald corridor that gave an easy flick to the heart of the green.

3

'That's one you don't want back,' said Root.

'They come off sometimes.'

Root was aware of a vague feeling of apprehension as he prepared to tee up his own ball. He took some time over the ritual of placing the brilliant white ball on its red plastic pedestal. There were days when you could walk up to the first tee, throw a ball on to the scarred surface and whack it away with the first wood you put your hand to. This wasn't one of them. He heard the unknown and unseen woman's laughter ringing out again. Parsons was at it to the last with the women. The pro had finally over-stepped the mark when he had carelessly dated two members' wives on the same evening.

Root took a quarter-swing a few inches from the ball. The wrists seemed to be relaxed. The hips moved fluidly enough, considering that he had been pounding a beat through outlying building sites for a good part of the previous night. Yet the feeling of insecurity remained. He felt as he often did in the toughest of the mining villages, a grim derelict place where youngsters still fought a battle against the colliery that had been won in the year of nationalization: the feeling that blind, mindless violence could erupt with appalling swiftness. He shook his head. It was the gritty rain that had spoiled his mood. Or maybe he had been piqued by Lecky's perfect tee-shot.

He fixed his eye on the little diamond on the new ball. It would be a full, hefty drive, delivered heartily and followed through with feeling. He swung back slowly, his left shoulder moving gradually to a point a few inches from his long chin. The diamond on the bright ball winked at him. He reached the top of his backswing.

Someone screamed.

Root swung wildly through the ball, catching it on the toe of the club and sending it whistling off high and right, where it was caught by a gust of wind and whipped away from the fairway to finish in the deepest patch of rough on the course.

Root began a curse and glared at the spinney where the noise had come from.

Lecky looked concerned.

'Bad luck,' he offered pacifically.

'Did he have to yell just then!'

'I watched it all the way. Bad luck. You might find it,' said Lecky.

Root knew it was a lost ball, but he managed a wry smile.

'Aye,' he agreed. 'But I'll play a provisional just in case.'

Root was about to place the new ball on the tee when another sound came from the spinney. It was as impatient and full of emotion as the high-pitched scream which had spoiled his drive. But this one made him freeze on the backswing.

'Murder !'

Two

'An "iron" club is one with a head which usually is relatively narrow from face to back, and usually is made of steel.'

Arthur Root had heard the cry before. He had been on patrol when a pair of teenagers in Gritmarsh had beaten another into a broken heap: they had skulked about for an hour, unable to stay away from the enormity of what they had done. It was not until a group of colliers returning from a late shift found the dead youth that they fled. Root had been trying doors and thinking of his medium-iron shots. He heard the hoarse shouts from the miners: *Murder!* The youths ran into him. White-faced in the starlight, black blood on their fluorescent shirts, they had been so astonished that they began to weep. Their aggression turned to gusty self-pity when they saw who held them, and they spoke of a vicious knife attack by a youth twice their size; of an unlucky blow and their dismay. They didn't try to break away. Root, a deceptively slim man, was known in the villages as more than useful if there was trouble.

'Murder?'

Root put the two-wood into his bag.

'Get the police!' called someone.

That was Frank Bell. Root knew his voice. He was Margaret Hughes' young man.

Root felt cold shivers spin along his back. Here? On the first at Wolvers? Then he recollected his duty. He moved quickly towards the direction of the shouting, plunging into the whippy undergrowth to the right of the first tee. Big drops of water flashed out at him. There was the sound of more voices. Everyone would want to see the corpse.

Root recollected with horror his first sight of the dead boy in the mean village street. It was the only murder he had seen in his twenty years of Yorkshire policing. Even then it had been at night, an almost casual killing. It had happened in a place that knew about crime.

There was something especially horrifying about the thought of violence at Wolvers. Of course there had been deaths at the club. Over there on the twelfth green, for instance, the most drunken dentist in the North of England, old Charlie Royal, had expired seconds after he watched his ball roll in for a birdie three. He had been smiling.

There had been almost a festive spirit. 'Charlie's snuffed it on the twelfth! Wish I could go like that – holed out for a three!' Members had grinned and joked. This wasn't a laughing matter.

Root called out in his night-duty voice. Sharp, clear and authoritative.

'Where are you?'

'Get the police!' Frank Bell called back. 'Dial 999!'

'I am the police!'

Then he saw them. A collection of Sunday morning golfers in the bright un-English colours. Margaret Hughes was behind him, bursting through the bushes. She usually turned up halfway through the morning to wait for Frank Bell. He wanted to tell her she'd get her feet wet. She hurled herself at Frank Bell.

'Stand back!' ordered Root. The Secretary was almost in tears. 'Come on, Mr Church, please. Phil. Stand away.'

'We want the police – an ambulance – a doctor! I sent for Dr Fordham. Didn't I? He's out somewhere on the course! Did someone send for the police?'

'I'm a policeman, Mr Church,' Root said. He guided the distraught man in the canary-yellow shirt away from the grim sight.

'What happened?'

'It's Tom,' said Frank Bell unnecessarily.

No one said what had happened.

'Who found him?'

'I did,' said Frank. 'Me and Phil. Des Purseglove's just gone to the phone. I didn't know you were out, Arthur.'

'That's all right, Frank. You did the right thing.'

'He's dead!'

The full force of the thing struck Root. Physical violence always unnerved him. He lived in a community which still talked of fist-fights as a sign of manhood. It was the part of the job he loathed. This was the ultimate waste. Unquestionably Tom Tyzack had been done to death. And there was no sign of the instrument that had killed him.

There were certain procedures to be followed. First you had to make sure there was nothing to be done for the victim. He found himself listening and prodding, all the while touching as little as possible. There was not a flicker of life in the big, sprawled body. Tyzack had been a cheerfully ugly man in life. Dead, he was a bogeyman. More people arrived to thrash about in the undergrowth and then shout harshly as they saw the corpse. It was very clear to all of them that Tyzack had died instantly. Any one of the wounds was enough to have broken the great, thick head.

'I had to make sure,' Root muttered.

'Yes!' Church was sobbing quietly. 'Get a doctor! They'll be around the far end – try the sixteenth! Joe Fordham went out second or third – tell him it's essential! Get him here!'

Root got to his feet. Margaret Hughes was clinging to Frank Bell as though he might be the next victim. She caught his eye and he could see that she understood how he felt. Tyzack had been a buffoon, a rich, prodigal man who was more boor than clown, a club character of little charm and considerable beastliness, but he was not a *thing* to be smashed and hacked at. It was outrageous.

Root slipped into the routine.

He moved the clustering onlookers back. The official things came easily now that he had a recognizable situation to deal with.

'Keep away!' he ordered. 'I'm taking charge, Mr Church. I want you to find the rest of the Committee and keep everyone here. Don't let anyone leave the club. Put a man or two on the car park. Go to the bar. Keep everyone here – tell them there's been an accident. You said Mr Purseglove went to get the police?'

'Yes! Yes!'

'Then get someone to meet the police cars.'

He began to take in the scene, memorizing every detail.

'Yes, yes, Arthur!' said Church. 'I'll go. Keep back, everyone – where's Dr Fordham! No one's to leave!'

'He's dead, isn't he?' said Frank Bell. Margaret was staring at the dead man.

Her pretty, tanned face had paled with shock. She looked like the child she had been when Root had first seen her, a defiant tot of two or three years who had come to inspect the new couple in the police-house. His wife had picked her up and dressed a graze on her knee. Ever since then, Margaret had been a source of delight to him; she was as dear to him and his wife as their own children.

'Take her away,' ordered Root. 'Go on, Margaret. There's nothing you can do. Go and help find Dr Fordham if you like. But don't come back. All of you.'

The small crowd of onlookers moved away reluctantly. By this time perhaps a couple of dozen golfers and caddies had arrived. There was a ball-scavenger as well. Normally no one would talk to the cloth-capped man who skulked in the rough, waiting for some un-fortunate golfer to lose his ball. Williamson, thought Root. 'Known to the police,' in the odd phrase: a petty thief. He remained in the background, wishing to see but not be noticed. No one paid him any attention.

It was then that Root realized that no murderer was about to rush into his arms and break down in tears. He looked at the circle of faces now at some distance away from the corpse. Half-hidden by the

9

springy bushes, they stared in glassy-eyed excitement at him. There was a killer nearby, he thought suddenly. It had to be someone on the course. But where was the murder weapon?

Root groaned aloud. A magpie swept clumsily through the birches. Blood seeped from the great wounds in Tyzack's skull. He wanted to cover up the corpse, but it wouldn't do. The rain had stopped and he might destroy evidence. Whatever happened now, he was not going to be able to golf on Sundays for some time. Not on Wednesdays. Nor early on Saturday mornings.

He heard more thrashings in the undergrowth. Frank Bell had found Fordham.

'Well, Arthur?'

He was seventy turned. He dressed almost exactly as Harry Vardon sixty years before, in tweed plus-fours and a collar and tie.

'If you'll look at Tom, please, Doctor.'

Fordham noted the official tone and was instantly the professional man.

'How long ago?'

'Five minutes. If you could avoid moving anything –'

'I know, I know!'

The examination was brief, almost instantaneous. Fordham got to his feet.

'He's dead. Nothing I can do. Bad business, Root. He was a useful golfer, though I can't say I cared for him. Who did it?'

'That will be the subject of an inquiry, sir.'

'It wasn't an accident.'

'No.'

Both knew this. But only Root was uneasy. Fordham had lived for fifty years with sudden death.

'It's murder.'

Fordham looked at Root speculatively. He was one of the few people who knew Root's state of mind. He had seen him at work, and he knew the policeman's hatred of causeless violence.

'You all right?'

'Yes, thanks.'

'Then I'll be off.'

10

The GP looked down at Tyzack's bull-like body. In death he looked even bigger than in life. 'Tom would have wanted us to finish the round.'

Root could grin at that.

'I'd rather you stayed, sir.'

'You know as well as I when he died. There's nothing I can do.'

Root heard the thin wailing of the police siren. He wondered when he'd be able to play golf again.

'Uncle Arthur!'

'Go to the clubhouse, Margaret,' Root ordered. 'Frank! I said keep her away!' He saw Lecky. 'Take Jack as well.'

Margaret persisted.

'I could ring Auntie Ursula. There's your dinner.'

Root realized that he would be on duty for the rest of the day, perhaps far into and through the night. Ursula was his wife. She and the children would not see him this Sunday. And his Sunday dinner – beef, puddings, sprouts, peas, potatoes and thick rich gravy – would be another sacrifice in the ritual of investigation.

'Aye, Margaret. Tell her I'll be late and I'll ring when I can.'

'It's murder, isn't it, Uncle Arthur?'

'Take her away, Frank.'

Margaret allowed Frank Bell to pull her through the unseen cluster of spectators. Root could hear their questions as she went towards the grey mansion. For the first time he considered his fellow-members, those who had come to view the body.

He felt the physical excitement of his kind. Without moving he began to look around the body. Tyzack had been killed. There was no weapon nearby.

He wondered if he had spoken to Tyzack's murderer.

Three

'. . . hazards should be distinctively marked.'

'Well it *is* murder, isn't it?' Margaret said again. She wished she had worn something warmer than the flimsy denim halter and skirt which Frank admired now that they were in the vastness of the club-house. It was more than the chill of the massive, thick-walled heap that made her feel cold. Along with Arthur Root and the rest of the playing members, the staff and the visitors at Wolvers that morning, she had come to realize that there was a killer at large. It disturbed her deeply. Margaret was a girl who had always instinctively been at pains to make her companions comfortable; yet now she felt shrewish. Frank wouldn't say a word. He had taken her arm and hauled her away from the spinney and then insisted that she sit in a corner of the big lounge far away from the noise and excitement of the bar. Jack Lecky had gone for the drinks.

'Frank, what did you see? I heard the scream — that was when poor Tom Tyzack must have been killed! Who was there? Did you say Mr Church found him? It must have been awful! And Uncle Arthur kept so calm! He'd got everybody away from the body in seconds – and he'd ordered us all off here! Frank, who did it?'

'I don't know!'

Ordinarily Frank Bell would have described himself as imperturbable. He was used to handling people and keeping their regard by his deft and tactful manner. He sold computers to steelmen who were somewhat in awe both of him as expert and of their own temerity in spending a couple of hundred thousand pounds when they had managed to get along quite nicely with a dozen clerks. It seemed frightful that Margaret should have seen the corpse – been present almost at the murder, for only the dense screen of half-grown birches and undergrowth stood between the first tee and the little hollow where Tyzack had been struck down. His hands shook.

'You're trembling, Frank!'

Margaret impulsively put his hands to her deep bosom in an entirely natural gesture. Lecky returned at that moment and Frank's embarrassment was complete.

The bar-lounge filled gradually and the chill was almost gone from the big room. As more of the seventy-odd golfers either completed or gave up their rounds, the noise increased. Margaret could see that the collar and tie rule had for once been abandoned. Men came straight from the locker-room to the bar.

'They're saying it must have been a scavenger,' Lecky said. 'A sort of unlucky accident when one of them was trying to get away with a stray ball.'

'It wasn't an accident,' Frank said. 'Not that.'

Margaret was conscious of a heightening tension. Men were coming in and calling questions at the others; sometimes one or another would point to Frank. Through the bay windows she could see the bright blue tent where the police car was parked. One of the uniformed crew returned to use the radio-telephone.

'So what happens now?' asked Margaret.

'We'll all be kept here,' Lecky said. 'Even if they find the murderer right away, there'll be questions. We're all witnesses, more or less.

13

We all heard the scream.'

'That scream!' said Margaret. 'And I thought it was someone yelling because he was angry at a bad shot!'

'It was Tom Tyzack,' said Frank Bell. 'I was quite near. We were all in the rough looking for my ball.' Margaret wanted him to keep quiet now that he was beginning to snap out of his horrified daze. But she couldn't bring herself to stop him. 'I sliced into the spinney. I very often do at that hole. I don't know why.' He was reliving the moment, and his wrist moved, flexing at the thought of the shot. 'If I hadn't sliced the ball, we wouldn't have gone into the spinney.'

'Frank!'

Margaret was appalled. Frank was blaming himself.

'It's true! I wanted that ball back! We all went to look for it. I was down at the bottom of the spinney – I didn't get a line because of the wind. It picked the ball up so quickly I'd hardly time to look up, though God knows I play enough shots with my head up at any other time!'

He broke off, for there was a lessening of the noise by the bar. Margaret saw the reason immediately. Jack Parsons, the short, square, brown-faced professional, had entered. With his usual over-elaborate gallantry he bowed from the waist as his pupil came through the door. It was she who would have invited him into the bar-lounge, for only by invitation could the pro enter. Parsons had been particularly unwelcome for the past three months. Today his presence was accepted without demur. If he chose to associate with Denise Steel, who should comment? A pig-faced woman of about forty, she radiated health, lust and enjoyment.

'Jack Parsons!' said Margaret indulgently. 'I didn't know he'd taken up with *her*!' Several of the members were talking to the couple. The Committee had attempted to ostracize him, but Parsons ignored the ban cheerfully.

Frank turned at the slight noise in the gravelled drive. A cream and gold ambulance had rolled up almost silently. It was followed by several police cars. The policemen got out quickly and made for the blue tent.

'They're here,' Frank added unnecessarily.

The bar loungers had seen the new arrivals. They crossed to the windows. The stewardess came too, followed by her morose husband.

'That's a man I couldn't take to,' said Jack Lecky, pointing to the steward, Charlie Bliss.

Frank Bell nodded. 'He's not liked. Why, what has he said now?'

'He didn't know the details till I was at the bar. Then that nice-looking wife of his told him Tyzack had been battered to death with a golf-club.'

'And?'

'All he said was, "How many strokes?".'

Margaret had been listening, though her attention was mainly on the new arrivals. She heard what Lecky said, however.

'He's a nasty piece of work!' she said. 'Nasty, creepy man! No wonder his wife – '

She stopped, for there was again one of those curious gaps in the blanket of noise in the lofty bar-lounge.

Into this silence Bliss called out:

'The poliss! I've seen that one before. Big man, Mabbatt, that's his name! Oh, some of you'll have to watch it now! Mabbatt's a right tight bastard!' Some of the crowd laughed; Bliss had his drinking companions amongst the members.

It was left to the pro, Parsons, to quieten him.

'Get back to your bar, Bliss, and give your mouth a rest. You make me sick!'

Bliss began to snarl an answer at the profesional, but Parsons' order was taken up by more of the excited, thirsty golfers. The steward laughed. Parsons watched him all the way to the bar.

'Mabbatt?' said Lecky. 'I've heard of him before. 'Wasn't he something to do with the immigrants in the sixties?'

'He settled the local gangs,' said Frank Bell. 'He's got a reputation for toughness.'

'He's big enough,' said Margaret.

Frank felt talk welling up inside him like a dammed stream. He was over the first shock of discovery. All he wished to do now was to

have Margaret to himself and let the words flow. But Lecky was there, so all he said was what everyone was beginning to wonder:
'Why should anyone want to kill Tom Tyzack?'

Four

'An "observer" is appointed ... to assist ... to decide questions of fact ...'

'I know you, don't I?'

'Yes, sir,' said Root.

He was back on the first tee, sick at heart and in great need of the beer that was being transferred from the bright blue tent to the thirsty golfers in the clubhouse. The rat-faced steward winked at Root, though he looked away as Mabbatt's ponderous head moved in his direction.

'I never forget a face,' Mabbatt said. 'I know you.'

'Sir.'

'PC Root,' said one of the CID men. Root couldn't recall his name. Sparker? Striker? Strachan? He had been a detective-constable at the time of the Gritmarsh killing. 'He was instrumental in apprehending the — '

'Don't tell me.' rumbled Mabbatt. 'I don't like clever buggers who're always trying to tell me things. Get this straight,' he said, addressing Root, the two CID men, Elaine, who wobbled daintily past with a tray of sparkling glasses, and assorted photographers, fingerprint men and stone-faced uniformed men torn from cricket matches, Sunday dinners and pubs to help in the tedious business of searching and interviewing. All gave him their attention. Mabbatt was famous for his dislikes. Pakistanis, queers, voyeurs, toy poodles, the new postage stamps, the press, his wife – all had incurred his wrath. They would continue to do so. Root waited for another dislike to be named, but Mabbatt had forgotten what he had intended to say. Elaine's elegant wobble disturbed him.

They watched and waited, but Mabbatt had turned to Root again.

'You sorted out the peepers in Hagthorpe.'

'No, sir.'

'No?'

Mabbatt was an immense man. He towered some four or five inches over Root, who did not consider himself small. Root's misery increased. Golf at Wolvers receded into a fainter distance, rather like the first on a November day. When mist shrouded the first green, it seemed to be a thing of the imagination which could never be reached by real golf-balls; so it was with his next game of golf. Mabbatt would turn all his spare time into reports, inquiries, and interviews.

'I can't remember you, but I know your face. Well?'

'Gritmarsh, sir. That Innes lad who was stabbed.'

Mabbatt had been Detective Chief Inspector of Division at the time.

'Knew I was right. Good thing you were on hand. Why were you here?'

'I'm a member, sir.'

Root tried to tone down the ring of satisfaction in his voice. Mabbatt was displeased again.

'One of this lot, eh? Hate this kind of crowd.'

Mabbatt's elevation to Detective Superintendent at District hadn't removed the old chip from his shoulder.

'Bring some of that beer!' he called to Elaine.

She giggled and rushed to obey.

18

'Well?' said Mabbatt, drinking deeply.

Root licked his lips, but the Superintendent's huge face showed no sign of compassion. Root suspected that golfing policemen were beginning to figure among his hates. He drew out his notebook.

'At ten-thirty-two on the morning of Sunday, July the –'

'Not that! Tell me what happened! You can get the speeches ready for the coroner. I want to know about *that*!'

'Sir.' Root thought of the thieves he had been trying to catch the night before. They made a business of stealing bricks. The problem was: how did they transport them? No one had heard or seen a vehicle. They couldn't carry them away. Surely not?

Mabbatt's conclusion was that Root had been surprisingly efficient. He came to a decision that would have completed Root's discomfiture.

'The body was found by Tyzack's partners, sir. They were Frank Bell, Desmond Purseglove and Philip Church. Mr Church is the Secretary.'

Mabbatt stared at Root, so he went on:

'I proceeded immediately I heard the shouts, sir.'

'And you sent for assistance?'

'I remained with the body, sir, and got the groundsmen to rope off the area. Mr Church had already sent for assistance.'

'Church, you say?'

'The Secretary, sir.'

'There was no one else about?'

Root did not let his bewilderment show. There had been dozens of people thrashing about in the undergrowth.

'Several, sir.'

'Names?'

'I made a list out, sir.' Root had already given the sheet to the Sergeant. It wasn't Striker. Not Strachan?

'I put a note of next-of-kin too, sir.'

'Here, sir,' said the young man.

'Why didn't I get this before, Strapp?'

Strapp. That was it.

'I was arranging interview rooms, sir. All ready when you are, sir.'

'Next-of-kin, who is it, wife?'

'Yes, sir.'

'She been told yet?'

'I don't think so, sir.'

'See to it, Sergeant.'

There would be time later to tell the Superintendent about Tyzack's domestic arrangements. Strapp quickly detailed a crew. Mabbatt waited for him to return.

'Who did it?'

Mabbatt barked the question at both men. Root watched the bubbles and foam in Mabbatt's empty glass. Could it be possible, he wondered, that things would be normal again? He found his voice:

'I'd say it was a golfer, sir.'

'Get Root a beer,' Mabbatt ordered. 'He's the only one who talks sense. Why?'

Root had spoken only after considerable reflection. It seemed blindingly obvious that a man who had been murdered in bright daylight on a golf course which was populated almost entirely by golfers could almost certainly be said to have suffered at the hands – or the club – of one of them. It had been very soon established that Tyzack had taken a club into the spinney with him; and that a pitching-wedge was missing from the expensive set in his golf-bag. Was Mabbatt serious?

'The injuries, sir. I'm making a deduction, that's all, sir, but it looked to me as though Tom Tyzack had been killed with a club.'

'That's what Dr Fordham said,' Mabbatt grunted. 'And the police surgeon. He's a golfer too. I wouldn't be surprised if –'

Mabbatt stopped.

'Here's your beer. This golf-stick?'

'Sir?'

'Why would he have it with him? He wasn't playing at the time.'

'To poke about with, sir. In the undergrowth. That's how you'd look for a ball – you'd always take a club with you.'

Mabbatt grunted.

'Why not one of the scroungers?'

'I can't see it, sir.' Mabbatt was sharper than he looked, far

20

quicker-witted than he allowed himself to appear. He must have talked to some of the members to have found out about the scavengers at Wolvers. 'We have this problem, like all golf courses. We can't keep out trespassers. If we were to put a dog on them, they'd take reprisals. Dig up the greens, break windows, smash the machines – it's happened at other places. So we have to put up with them. We could get them for stealing, but the Committee won't let me do anything. There's about a dozen of them, oldish men usually. One or two with convictions. That one' – Root pointed to a name on the list – 'Williamson. He was fined for stealing bees a few years back. He must make three or four pounds a week. They sell the balls. Five or ten pence for a good ball, less for one that's cut.'

Root paused. Mabbutt was listening, his big head cocked on one side so that he could watch the progress of the search. It had been organized meticulously. A gaunt plain-clothes man with a Geordie accent was in charge. Root didn't know him, but he approved of his methods. The Geordie had obtained from Parsons a club similar to the one missing from Tyzack's bag. Each of the searchers had seen it. Each had his instructions. Look for blood, for signs of cleansing – clumps of grass torn out, blood-stained leaves, soil disturbed by the axe-like blade of the murder weapon. And especially for the missing wedge.

'Anything wrong?' asked Mabbatt. 'Say if there is. You were Johnnie-on-the-spot. You could have seen something my lads missed.'

'It's not that, sir. I thought I'd been talking for a long time.'

'You think that's talking for a long time? You should know better, Root!'

'Sir. I couldn't see any of the scavengers killing Tom Tyzack. They'd all know him well enough to help him look for a ball. He was always on the course. A low-handicap man.'

'Good?'

'Good and keen, sir.'

'And that's why it wasn't a scavenger?'

'No, not that, sir. It isn't too easy to explain, but Tom was more their kind than most members here.'

'How?'

'He'd come up the hard way, Tom. And he was a local man. Any of the scroungers would know that Tom wouldn't do much if he caught them. He might shout a bit or even fetch them one across the ear. They'd accept that. But you wouldn't get the *viciousness* from a scavenger. And there's another thing, sir. About Williamson.'

'Well?'

'Can we have him over.'

Mabbatt stared.

'Aye.'

He turned to Sergeant Strapp.

'Get him, Sergeant.'

They waited.

Root watched the search developing. He cast his mind back to the scene of Tyzack's death. Was there anything else he could tell Mabbatt? *No.* There had been too many people too quickly. Accidents always brought an audience, murder the biggest. So many people so quickly!

Williamson recognized Root:

'Hello, Mr Root, sir!'

'Hello, Sam. I want you to help us. This is Superintendent Mabbatt.'

''Eard on you, sir.'

'Aye! You were there, Williamson – doing what?'

'Told the Sergeant already.'

'So you were scrounging, were you?'

Williamson's rheumy eyes showed resentment but no fear. South Yorkshiremen had a disdain for authority that was unmatched in England.

'I were after a golf-ball or two, aye! What on it?'

Root saw that Mabbatt's ire could break out at any moment. To forestall a crisis, he said:

'Sam, roll your shirt-sleeves up.'

Mabbatt's large face flushed.

'Right, Mr Root,' said Williamson.

He struggled, but Root had to help him. Mabbatt watched coldly.

22

He saw why Root had intervened. The arms were cruelly mis-shapen.

'He got this in a pit accident, sir,' said Root.

'Trapped eight hours,' said Williamson. 'But I wouldn't let doctors cut 'em off.'

Mabbatt regained control of himself. He was learning new things about Root. He was more than an ordinarily competent village bobby. Root was deeper than most, yet there was a quality about him that Mabbatt reacted against : *softness*. Though he admitted Root's intelligence, Mabbatt found his humanity irritating.

Root, for his part, found Mabbatt's approach crude. You didn't talk to anyone like this. Not even a petty criminal who made a living from scavenging.

'So you saw the golfers in the spinney ?' he said to Williamson.

'Aye.'

'Anyone else ?'

Williamson's narrow face set into a scowl, much like Mabbatt's.

'No! Like I told Sergeant !'

Mabbatt dismissed him.

'You got a full statement ?' he asked Strapp.

'Yes, sir.'

'So he's out of it,' said Mabbatt to Root.

'I'd think so, sir.'

'You'd think right.'

Root watched Williamson merging into the bushes like a shadow. The scrounger might have been more forthcoming with a bit of persuasion ; it was obvious that he had clammed up when Mabbatt had shown his anger.

He shrugged. He wasn't CID.

'Now,' said Mabbatt. 'Root, you kept your eyes open. Facts.'

'There were around seventy people out on the course at the time of the murder, sir. We can eliminate most of them because they were in full view of a number of witnesses at the time of the murder. Some we can't.'

Mabbatt turned to the thickset sergeant.

'Arrange for Root to be detached.'

To Root he said, 'Anything you can't leave?'

Root thought about the thirty or forty 'cases' which made up the working life of any village policeman. They ranged from complaints of litter-dumping to small-scale but persistent thieving.

'They're all in the book, sir. I can fill in the details for whoever takes over.'

'Then that's settled. Keen on this place, aren't you?'

'You could say that, sir.'

'You'll see plenty of it in the next few days.'

Root's unhappiness deepened. His long, brown face took on a look of complete dejection. There was nothing worse than being on a golf course when there was not the remotest possibility of playing.

Five

'When a round is cancelled, all penalties incurred in that round are cancelled.'

Most of the Committee had remained sober. Only Philip Church was noticeably affected.

Elaine Bliss pretended to listen to him.

'We have to decide about the morning's play! Does it stand or doesn't it? More than half completed the round, and they want to know!'

'I shouldn't let it worry you, Mr Church.'

'But Dr Fordham wants to know! He and his partner put in a gross eight-one – net sixty-nine! They're almost certain to win!'

'He won't be all that bothered right now, will he?'

It was almost beyond her comprehension that this man, a powerful industrialist, one of the richest men in South Yorkshire, should be so daunted by the simple task of telling his fellow-members that they would have to wait for the results of the morning competition. At fifty, he looked like a bland and nerveless thirty-five. His cheeks glowed with health, his white hair shone, and he held his short, fat body erect. And yet he trembled at the thought of making a simple decision.

'No! No, that's not the way to organize a competition! I took this job on and I said I'd carry it out! Excuse me! I'll catch Harry Tufnell! And Des Purseglove!'

He hurried away.

'How much longer will they keep us?' asked Parsons. He was addressing no one in particular. His pupil giggled.

'I'm enjoying it! I haven't had so much fun here since last Christmas when my old man fell down the stairs. Frank, have they caught him yet?'

Denise Steel pushed a five-pound note into the pro's hand. She dripped gold and diamonds.

'Go on, get me another. And Frank. Big ones. Now, love, don't stand there staring. Go behind the bar yourself if that little swine won't serve you.'

Parsons liked the idea. He slipped through the crush. Denise pushed her big breasts into Frank Bell's midriff.

'Well?'

'They haven't arrested anyone, no.'

'Why not! Everyone says it was that nutter who pinches bees — why don't they handcuff him and let us all go home? I mean, I'd stay here all day, Frank, but some of the others want to get away. And Churchie says we're here for the afternoon.'

'I think we are.' said Frank.

Sandwiches arrived on the bar, but before he could reach out for a plateful they had all vanished.

'I can't be any faster!' Elaine called. 'I'm cutting them as quick as I can!'

Bliss appeared, but he was far too excited to serve drinks. He squinted at his drinking cronies. Frank watched but he could barely hear through the noise.

'Clubs!' he heard. 'Clubs!'

The word passed quickly, and there was comparative quiet whilst

Bliss was made to repeat his piece.

'It's true – that's what they're doing! I saw them at it – they're wheeling all the sets of clubs to the back of the clubhouse! All of them!'

'You know what that's for,' said one member. 'They're looking for blood! I dare say there'll be traces.'

'They've no right –' began Church. He stopped. It struck him how ludicrous he must sound. Surprisingly, the realization gave him a sort of desperate courage. 'I've ruled this morning's play cancelled!'

'Good,' said Parsons returning. 'I won't have to check the cards. That gives me a bit of time in hand. Eh, Denise?' He patted her neat backside.

'You dirty dog!' screamed Denise Steel.

Frank acknowledged the drink, downed some of it and gave up the hunt for sandwiches.

'You go for the sandwiches, Margaret,' he said. 'Please.'

'All right.'

She saw that he was unsteady.

'Frank, what's wrong?'

'Nothing. It's just the whole rotten business. Tom Tyzack. And now they're examining everyone's clubs.'

'Are they!' whistled Lecky.

'Well there goes Tom!' called someone.

The noise stopped.

A man called Aspinall raised his glass as the ambulance bearing Tom Tyzack's body swirled away, kicking up spurts of gravel from the drive.

'Cheers, Tom!' One or two more joined in the toast.

Philip Church's voice rang out again:

'Get a screw-driver, Bliss! Hurry!'

'What's going on, Phil?' called several people.

Church was standing before the large-scale map of the course.

'The police want it! And no one's to leave! Please!'

'Then get some more beer!' called Parsons. 'I'm not staying here all afternoon without a drink!'

Church trembled but ignored him.

Bliss took the glass-framed map down. He pointed to the spinney and made a cross.

'*X* marks the spot, eh!'

Several of his cronies laughed, for he winked and made a grimace as if to suggest secret knowledge.

'I wish they'd done you instead,' said Parsons. 'At least Tom was a man.'

Six

'... the players shall refer any dispute to the Committee.'

Mabbatt watched the Secretary struggling with the big map. He was waiting to hear from the District Assistant Chief Constable. Soon, every kind of County Force brass-hat would be hovering around.

But the immediate things had been done. Now, sitting in the roomy mobile police headquarters, with its phone extensions, wireless, typewriters, maps and desks, he could watch the progress of the inquiry. A uniformed Inspector was setting a Task Force to work. They would be deployed about the course to keep sightseers away and guard the scene of the crime. The pathologist had arrived, and the coroner was expected. Laboratory assistants were waiting to take samples of soil, undergrowth, blood. The impressive resources of a big Force were on display.

'Now, Superintendent, I've brought the map!' puffed Church.

'Thank you, sir,' said Mabbatt.

'What can I tell our members? How long will you need them?'

He had calmed considerably after making the pronouncement about the morning's play; it seemed to him quite wonderful that no one had protested about the possible loss of the awards – three golf-balls each for the winners of the Better-Ball Medal round, and about five pounds made up of members' entry stakes.

'I shan't keep them any longer than necessary, sir.' said Mabbatt. 'You'll appreciate that there are certain steps that have to be taken immediately?'

'What steps?'

Mabbatt looked over Church's head.

'I'd like statements from your members.'

'All of them! What, today?'

'I'm sure you'll wish to help us with our inquiries?'

'Of course. But we can't stay here all day! I mean, many of us have commitments. I myself have an engagement to speak this evening at the Aldermanic Hall.'

'Then we'll take your statement immediately, sir. Sergeant Strapp!'

A worried look came over his face once more and he relapsed into his earlier state of confusion. 'There'll be sightseers! I'll have to tell the Head Greenkeeper to keep them out.'

Strapp knew how to handle Church.

'We'll look after that, sir. There'll be a guard on the course at all times. We'll be around for a while.'

Root silently agreed. From what he had seen, the investigation would take days. The trouble was that there were too many suspects. What had at first seemed a simple matter had become a knotty problem of topography and numbers.

'Let's get down to it,' Mabbatt ordered when Church allowed Sergeant Strapp to take him away.

A police artist was completing an enlarged map of the section of the course where the murder had been committed. He worked with brisk strokes, summoning up undergrowth, spinney, fairways and bunkers, greens, tees, isolated ancient trees and the single red cross that meant the place which ever afterwards would be shunned by the younger and more impressionable caddies. What would they call it? Death Corner? Ghost Spinney? Root found himself dreaming as

30

Mabbatt and he watched the artist step back and consider his work.

'That do, sir?'

'It'll do.' Mabbatt felt the drawing. 'Is it dry?'

'Yes, sir. The ink dries at once.'

Root could not warm to Mabbatt, but he began to admire his brusque efficiency. He hadn't actually done anything, apart from walk around the area covered by the map. Strapp had written a press hand-out. The gaunt Geordie – a detective sergeant, Root learned – had conducted the so far fruitless search in the spinney. Another experienced officer was examining the bags of golf-clubs. Mabbatt left the groundwork to others. Yet the investigation took shape around him.

'Take notes,' Mabbatt told a uniformed constable behind Root. 'Get it all typed up as soon as you can. Now, Root. Show me.'

'This is the way we went, sir. There's the tent, backing onto the spinney.'

'What's the idea of that – beer nearer the course?'

'Yes, sir. There's a club rule that states members have to change before going into the bar. Having the tent out here means they can get a drink immediately they've finished playing. Quite a lot of members have one or two beers, then they go to the locker-rooms.'

'It's there every week?'

'Throughout the summer, sir.'

Mabbatt pointed to the spinney. 'We started at the tent. Then on to this – what is it, tee?'

'The first tee, sir. Where I was standing.'

'Looking almost due north.'

Mabbatt traced the outline of the spinney. It was bounded on the west by the first fairway, and on the east by the second fairway. The northern side was marked by tufts of grass in the artist's felt-tip pen: the semi-rough. And the southern boundary of the spinney was covered almost entirely by the same kind of short rough alongside the ninth green. The effect was of a kidney-shaped area, neatly decorated with tiny trees, surrounded on all sides by ink-washed green.

'Area approximately eighty yards west-east by seventy-five north-

31

south,' Mabbatt said. 'Body found almost in the centre of the spinney. Persons so far known to be in the spinney at the time of the crime are the three other members of the – team?'

'Called a fourball, sir. Two play against two.'

'Aye. Others known to be in the immediate area. This Williamson. The professional and a woman. The steward.' He broke off. To the Geordie sergeant who had just entered he called, 'Well?'

'Nothing, sir.'

'Keep them at it till dark.'

'Very good, sir.'

'Right, Root. Talk.'

They had walked around the spinney earlier together, pin-pointing the exact position of the people who had been on the course at the time of the scream. Mabbatt wanted the events sharp and clear. He wanted to look from every possible angle at the wet little copse, so that he could later read through the mass of statements with a complete knowledge of the topography. His thoroughness evoked Root's professional admiration.

Root talked, but his mind was on that unhurried survey earlier.

'The spinney was under direct observation from all sides at all times immediately before and after the crime,' he began. 'Groups of golfers were proceeding along the first and second fairways, so that the west, east and northern sides were covered by sight witnesses. The southern side was under observation by two groups of golfers, one group on the twelfth fairway, and another on the twelfth tee.'

The crime was becoming one of those familiar problems that Root was constantly facing – like the niggling thefts. Someone with a unique form of transport had stolen the bricks. Find the transport, catch your man. Here the circle of suspects was narrowing. As he had walked alongside Mabbatt down the first fairway, he had felt the thrill of the hunt taking hold of him. Find the man who couldn't be accounted for by the other golfers and you caught your murderer; convict him by finding the murder weapon.

At first it had seemed so straightforward that Root believed they would make an arrest that day. He had put to the back of his mind the thought that he might have to help in the apprehension of a

32

friend. Doubt had set in very soon. It was true that Root himself could say categorically that no one could have entered the spinney from the west during the ten minutes or so he had stood on the first tee with Lecky. Similarly, Cathcart and his crew would be able to recall if anyone had crossed their path in their slow progress down the first. The four on the second tee, and the four in front of them who had reached the bunkers on the second fairway could agree that no one had cut across them into the spinney. The same applied to the south, with even more witnesses.

It seemed that the whole of the north, south, west and east sides were effectively a *cordon sanitaire*.

It was a stimulating puzzle at first.

Gradually, and with some skill, Root set the scene. When he had finished, the crime and its setting took shape. The uniformed constable taking notes already had decided which of the possible suspects in the green arena had committed the murder. Root and Mabbatt, much older men, were turning from a consideration of opportunity to motive.

'So they all rushed to see what was happening?'

'Most of them, sir. Mr Cathcart and his companions carried on playing. They didn't learn of the death until twenty minutes later.'

Mabbatt and Root were thinking the same thing. If only more of the players had stayed where they were after the crime, the investigation would be that much easier. There were numerous vantage points on the first few holes at Wolvers. From the tees on the first, the third and the fourth it had been possible for Mabbatt and Root to see almost the whole of the spinney.

'We want that golf-stick,' said Mabbatt. 'It's out there somewhere. Who's got it?'

Murderer and murder weapon: the two were interlinked. One would lead to the other. It wasn't as though they were looking for a small object, thought Root. An iron was a substantial instrument. You couldn't simply walk away with a thing like that.

But someone had.

'Let's see what your pals have to say,' said Mabbatt.

Seven

'If the player's ball be touched or moved by an opponent ... that opponent shall incur a penalty ...'

Frank Bell had drunk far more than he intended. So had most of the members, who were working through the more esoteric of the stocks of whisky now that the normal brands had been consumed. Frank chewed on a ham sandwich and listened to Lecky and Margaret. She was talking about him.

'He was an oddity at school. It wasn't that he was different. He played football and he had friends. It was this sort of – remoteness. He was always absolutely entranced by his work. The rest of us might have been a million miles away. Of course I knew I was going to marry him, even then.'

She grinned at Frank.

'He's a lucky man,' said Lecky sincerely. 'Hello? What's this?'

A uniformed constable was asking questions at the bar. Bliss wriggled forward, rat-faced smile ready. He pointed to the corner

34

where they sat. The policeman moved towards them as Lecky spoke. 'Mr Bell, is it, sir?'

'Yes.'

'Superintendent Mabbatt would like to see you, sir.'

'Don't worry,' Margaret said.

He bit back a retort. Margaret had the habit of managing him. It had never irritated him before.

'All right.'

Mabbatt had just been interviewed by his superior, the Assistant Chief Constable of Division. The Chief Constable had been making inquiries, though he wouldn't be calling in. However, he would expect a quick arrest. Mabbatt knew enough not to commit himself to a promise, though he felt he would soon settle the Wolvers case.

Frank was surprised to see Root with Mabbatt. He almost said 'Hello, Arthur,' but he noted Root's stiff bearing. Root nodded.

'Hello, Frank. This is Superintendent Mabbatt.'

Mabbatt was unimpressed. Frank was only just regulation size, and with his eyesight he would have been unacceptable to the Force. He looked half-drunk.

'Routine, this, sir,' Mabbatt assured him. 'You're a vital witness.'

'There's not much I can tell you.'

'Why not?'

Frank shook his head.

'I suppose because I didn't see much.'

'You began playing at what time?'

'I suppose about nine.'

'You always played with the dead man?'

'No. Not always. But we fixed this game last week. Phil Church and me against Tom and Des Purseglove.'

'It was you who discovered the body?'

'Yes.'

'Was Thomas Tyzack a quarrelsome man?'

'Yes – in a way – why do you – '

'Let me ask the questions, sir.'

'I was only going to say that he had a temper, but he wasn't quarrelsome in the sense that he'd look for trouble.'

35

'You're what age, sir?'

'Twenty-three.'

'And your profession?'

'I'm in computers. I'm a systems engineer.'

'How long have you been a member of the club?'

'About seven years.'

'And you've known the deceased for the whole of that time?'

Frank began to feel a dull pain behind his eyes. There was an air of hostility about the big man. It wasn't so much his pig's eyes that disturbed you; it was more the sheer weight of the huge head as it moved slowly and fractionally.

'I suppose so.'

'And you know him as a quarrelsome man?'

'No! I didn't say that!'

'Did any other member of your party have a dispute with him?'

Frank realized that it was too much. He shook his head free of the alcohol fumes.

'I'm not sure you've a right to ask that.'

'I have, sir. I have!'

There was a pause. Frank gave in.

'Tom Tyzack quarrelled over every hole in every game he ever played. He said the caddie sneezed or that someone was playing out of turn or that someone hadn't scored all their shots or *anything*! He'd throw his club at a blackbird or a rabbit. He was like a big child.'

'Thank you, sir.'

Root saw that he was enjoying himself. For the life of him he couldn't see what was happening; why should Mabbatt wish to rattle a decent lad like Frank Bell?

Frank went on without further questions.

'Tom was his usual self. He said he wouldn't play if Phil took a caddie along, so he didn't. He told Des Purseglove that he'd broken the rules by teeing up his ball in front of the Medal markers on the fourth tee. And he told me I'd deliberately put my shadow across his line when he was putting on the third green. Nobody minded very much. You see, you put up with people.'

Root nodded. It was true. Non-golfers wouldn't know. They didn't understand the saying that it never rains on golf courses; that there is no such thing as bad golfing weather. – In the same way, there's no one you couldn't play golf with.

'That's very helpful, Mr Bell.'

Mabbatt let his big head sink to the desk. He smiled almost benevolently at Frank. Then he let a golf-ball roll towards the young man. Frank caught it to stop it rolling off the table.

'Recognize this, sir?'

'It's my ball!'

'That's right, sir.'

Root watched. It seemed a very ordinary golf ball. It was new, white and lettered. Seeing it brought back a half-memory, however. Hadn't Margaret Hughes said something about a paint Frank was working on?

'Well – where did you find it?'

'You recognize it as yours?'

Frank was halfway between bewilderment and discomfort.

'Yes – there's my name.'

'So it is, sir. So it is.'

Frank's face was almost red.

'It's a special ball. We were looking in the rough. I sliced it and a gust of wind took it right into the spinney.'

'It isn't usual for a ball to have the owner's name sir?'

'No. It was one of six I printed over myself. I was sure it was in the spinney – did your men find it?'

Mabbatt disregarded the question.

'You said this was a special ball, sir?'

'Yes!'

Frank began to stammer:

'I'm – that is, I do – I go in for – I suppose I'm an inventor. I'm trying to develop a findable lost golf-ball!' Frank saw the incomprehension on Mabbatt's face. 'It's an invention. I'm trying to develop a new kind of paint.'

Root stared. So that was Frank's paint! A findable golf-ball! He remembered the attempts not many years before of a well-known golf-ball manufacturer to impregnate balls with radio-active materials so that they could be found by a locating device. The trouble was the cost. It wasn't justified. Losing golf-balls occasionally was cheaper. Could it be that Frank had discovered something more practicable?

'And this is it, sir, is it?'

'It must be – you found it, didn't you!'

'Oh, yes, we found it, sir.' He paused. 'It was in Mr Tyzack's jacket pocket.'

Frank let the ball slip from his fingers.

'Now, sir, how did it get there?'

The rest of the interview was a blur to Frank Bell as he returned to the bar. His mind was in a turmoil. Mabbatt had dodged from question to question, always returning to the central points. What had Frank seen, why should Tyzack put the ball in his pocket, what business contacts had he with Tom Tyzack, had there been a quarrel between him and Tom – his dejection showed so much that he was greeted with ribald inquiries as he returned to the bar. Bliss winked at his cronies and muttered something. Frank was a most unhappy and angry young man.

Root watched as Mabbatt stared at the golf-ball.

'There'd be money in this?'

'I just don't know, sir.'

'Think, Root! What do you think I took you on for – I want you to think golf and murder! Suppose this lad came up with his findable ball?'

'It would be worth a bob or two, sir.'

'And Tyzack would know this?'

Root said nothing.

'We'll find out more about Mr Tyzack, Root, and that before long. Now, look at this statement from your Secretary.'

Root obeyed. It was the familiar kind of thing. Not over-long, as some statements tended to be. Sergeant Strapp knew his business.

'Well?'

'Not helpful, sir.'

There was the necessary information, of course. Where and when, who and what, Church's actions on finding Frank with the corpse.

'There.'

Root looked at the indicated line. Philip Church had stated: 'Frank Bell was very annoyed at the loss of his ball. We'd spent more than the usual five minutes looking for it, and I thought we should be off.'

'Yes, sir,' said Root. 'I can't say I'd be very happy about losing a new ball.' He thought about the one he had sliced into the rough that morning. He would have no chance of searching for it.

Mabbatt's big head turned. 'It'll keep. Let's see this randy professional of yours.'

Parsons was palpably lit up.

'Hello – found your murderer yet?'

'I understand that you are under notice of dismissal, Mr Parsons.'

The little pro's brown face showed no sign of unease.

'Well, you know how it is – sometimes your face doesn't fit. What's that got to do with it?'

'Did I say it had, sir?'

'Come off it, man! I know how you coppers work! You want to needle a man, to make him feel he's muck! Well, try it! You can't touch Jack Parsons!'

'Exactly where were you at ten-thirty this morning, sir?'

'Where I always take a beginner – below the spinney in the dip between the first and second fairways. Nothing wrong with it. The club let me use that space.'

'You weren't in the spinney, sir?'

'I was giving a lesson.'

Root remembered the giggling.

'So you were outside the spinney?'

'Yes.'

'With your pupil, sir?'

'Yes!' He began to realize the nature of Mabbatt's questions.

'With a Mrs Steel, wasn't it, sir?'

Mabbatt's dislike showed. Root had been warned of the Superintendent's domestic problems. What he didn't know was that

Mabbatt's wife had left him for a quiet schoolteacher during a holiday in Majorca. Parsons sensed the massive hostility, though he too couldn't know the cause of it. Mabbatt detested philanderers.

'Yes. Denise was with me.'

'But not all the time?'

'No! She was near, though. She didn't want to go in the spinney. It was wet. Bloody wet!'

'So you went into the spinney?'

'So what if I did?'

'Alone, sir?'

'I suppose so!'

Parsons was distinctly uncomfortable.

'You heard the dead man's scream?'

Parsons tried to recapture his confident air.

'Everyone heard it.'

Mabbatt breathed morosely and heavily in the silence.

'Did you know that Mr Tyzack voted for your dismissal?'

Parsons looked older, and Root remembered the two young children and the sickly wife he had abandoned some years before. He was an unadmirable man.

'What if he did?'

'You were a friend of Mr Tyzack's, weren't you, sir?'

'Sort of. In his own way he was likeable enough.'

'Is there anything else you wish to tell me, sir?'

There was. It showed in the little pro's bearing. But he did not take up Mabbatt's challenge. His shoulders went back and the angry obscenities hovered unsaid.

Mabbatt said suddenly:

'What do you know about findable golf-balls, sir?'

'Good players buy them.'

Mabbatt frowned.

'That's all, then, sir. Sergeant Strapp will take your statement.'

Parsons grinned at Root.

'Try a wider arc on the backswing, Arthur. You'll get more distance.'

Root visualized his own impeccable, sturdy swing. He thought he might try the wider arc. When Parsons had gone with Strapp, he asked:

'How did you know about the voting, sir?'

He himself hadn't known which of the Committee had voted for Parsons' dismissal. Only that there had been a large majority.

'That steward keeps his ears and eyes open,' Mabbatt said. 'He's a creepy little sod, but he knows what's going on. Now, what do you know about this Purseglove?'

Root was startled.

'You want to see himself, sir? I thought he was — '

'Out of the running?'

Mabbatt got to his feet. He pointed to the green spinney. The artist had peopled it.

'Parsons there,' he said, indicating a tiny painted figure. 'He says he saw only the scrounger Williamson. He heard nothing till Frank Bell called out. Williamson claims he'd hidden to the west side of the spinney because he thought he might get a thump if he ran into Tyzack. There.' The scrounger was there to the life, a cloth-capped dark-suited blob. 'Bell near the body. Church with him. Both of them looking for the ball that Tyzack already had in his pocket. So they say. That leaves Bliss in the tent. There.' The police artist had let himself go over Bliss's face. He looked a feral thing, more animal than man. 'And the fourth member of the quartet in the clear. Not in the spinney at all.'

'Yes, sir.'

'Why not?'

'Sir?'

Mabbatt said impatiently:

'Why wasn't the fourth member of the game looking in the bloody shrubbery, Root?'

Root realized that he had accepted the obvious. Whilst the position of each player on the course was being plotted from the information so far available, he had not noticed this departure from golfing etiquette. Everyone looked for a lost ball. Next time, it might be your own.

'Well?'

'I couldn't say, sir. It isn't usual.'

'It isn't usual for a man to be hacked to death on a Sunday morning, is it, Root? Two witnesses say they saw Purseglove by his golf-trolley just there. He was there at the time of the yell. Why wasn't he in *there*!'

Purseglove's neat red-jacketed figure glowed.

'You're going to ask him, sir?'

'I'll see his statement.'

'Yes, sir.'

Mabbatt pointed to another figure, that of the stewardess.

'Another thing. Strapp's interview with the Bliss woman. Why should she turn all coy when Tyzack's name comes up?'

Bliss kept his job by not remarking on the distribution of his wife's favours. Root remembered saying as much to Jack Lecky only that morning.

'It's the same with most of the Committee, sir. Elaine Bliss is something of a Committee-man's perk.'

'Tyzack's on the Committee?'

'Yes, sir.'

'Tyzack? Him and the stewardess?'

'There was talk, sir.'

'Talk! I want to know!'

'It's fairly certain, sir.'

Mabbatt regarded the map again. He allowed his big finger to rest on the pert heavy-topped figure of Elaine Bliss, still smiling and still carrying her tray of glasses.

'Who were the others?'

'There's Freddie Sutton, sir.'

'I don't remember a Sutton.'

'He's away, sir. On business. He goes to America for months at a time.'

'That's three.'

'Then there's Mr Church,' said Root. He hesitated. 'I don't think he's been in the running since he became Secretary.'

Mabbatt shook his massive head slowly.

'You wouldn't credit it,' he said. 'You wouldn't, really. It's all the

Committee?'

'Not all, sir. The Captain, Harry Tufnell, never bothered. At least I don't think so.'

'And Bliss takes it!'

'It's a case of having to, sir. He wouldn't last long if Elaine didn't keep the Committee sweet. It's an arrangement that suits them both. Elaine's quite fond of associating with well-to-do men. Bliss wouldn't want to have to look for work. He calls this a bobby's job.'

Mabbatt was unamused.

'Church holds off now he's Secretary, eh?'

'His wife tends to be down here quite a lot. She's organizing the Captain's Dance next week.'

'Anyone else?' Mabbatt growled.

'Des Purseglove, sir. At least, he was one of them a couple of years back. He's an old Committee man.'

Mabbatt stared at the red-anoraked figure.

'Find him. And bring his statement.' He called Root back. 'And order some tea!'

Root was about to enter the bar when he heard the sudden uproar of driven-out breath.

A uniformed constable who was a stranger to him poked his head out of the smoke-filled bar.

'You're Root, aren't you?'

'Yes.'

'Come and sort this lad out, will you?'

Root went into the big room. Everyone was talking, describing, explaining, arguing: the cause of the noise was plain.

Bickerdike was holding a furious Frank Bell. The gaunt sergeant was a large, muscular man, but he was having trouble with Frank.

'Easy, Frank!' Root called. 'Steady!'

'Will you be sensible!' growled Bickerdike. 'Are you going to behave?'

Margaret was yelling much the same thing.

'What's happened?' Root asked. 'Frank – calm down!'

Frank subsided when he saw Arthur Root. The bright angry glare changed to hoplessness.

'He belted him one. Him.'

Root followed the direction of Bickerdike's nod. The steward lay half-supported by his cronies. Frank must have hit him very hard. His nose and mouth dripped blood.

'Couldn't have done it better myself,' said Parsons.

'Go and sit down, Frank,' ordered Root. 'Let him go now. He's all right. Margaret – you look after him.'

'He said something about Tom,' Frank muttered between clenched teeth. 'He said we needn't look far for the killer.'

'He'll be all right now,' said Root.

'Keep an eye on the lad will you?' said Bickerdike to Margaret Hughes. 'Don't let him make it a habit.'

Frank allowed Margaret Hughes to take him away.

Elaine Bliss entered as the steward staggered to his feet.

'Charlie!' she cried. 'You've hurt yourself!'

Bliss grinned through the blood. 'You know I wouldn't do that, love.'

'I'll put a stitch in,' said Fordham, crossing to the bar for his whisky. To Elaine Bliss he said, 'Try to keep him quiet. I mean, try to stop him passing remarks. There's been enough violence around here.'

Frank Bell was quiet in the corner, so Root ordered tea and sandwiches for himself and Mabbatt. Just then, Church called for attention:

'I've been to see the officer in charge of the inquiry,' he said crisply. 'He is satisfied that he has all the information he requires. He says we can all go home.'

'Lovely!' said Denise Steel. She hooked herself firmly onto the pro's arm and led him away.

For a moment Root included himself in the dismissal. Then he recalled that he was more than a member of the club. It had already been a crowded day, and there was no sign that he would be released before nightfall. If then.

He stopped Des Purseglove; no one overheard him.

'Not you, Des,' he said. 'Superintendent Mabbatt wants a word.'

'Me? I thought Phil said it was all over?' Purseglove looked worried. 'I'd like to be home soon. What is it? I told your Sergeant all I could remember.'

He was a meticulous dresser in a fairly shabby way; a neat respectable man, thought Root.

'It's only routine,' he said comfortingly. 'Come on. He'll not keep you.'

'I have to get home!'

But already they were being pushed to the door by the members. Mabbatt read Purseglove's statement as he sipped his tea.

'Now, Mr Purseglove,' Mabbatt said at last, raising the monstrous head from the page. 'Enjoy your golf?'

Purseglove swallowed, and Root felt sorry for him.

'Enjoy – '

'I thought that was the idea,' Mabbatt said, adopting a puzzled tone.

'But poor Tom was – '

'Murdered.' Mabbatt let the word make its impact. 'So it's important to remember everything you saw or heard, sir.' Mabbatt went on in a return to his confidential style: 'We'd appreciate your co-operation, Mr Purseglove.'

'And you shall have it!' Purseglove burst out. 'Without reserve!'

'Right. Why weren't you looking for the lost golf-ball.'

'I was!'

'So you were in the spinney?'

Purseglove looked around to Root and then to the map on the wall. He seemed to draw confidence from his inspection.

'Let's get this clear, Superintendent,' he began firmly.

'Take your time, sir.'

Root did not admire the technique, but he knew it to be effective. Disrupt apparent confidence. Introduce self-questioning, so that the witness examined his own recollections of events. But Purseglove was not disturbed.

'All right. I'll tell you what I told the Sergeant.'

'Sergeant Strapp,' said Mabbatt, looking down at the statement.

'I told him,' Purseglove said steadily, 'that I helped look for the ball for a few minutes, then I wanted a cigarette. So I went for one.'

Mabbatt nodded.

'Very clear, sir. Hadn't Mr Tyzack got one?'

Purseglove smiled.

'Tom never gave anything away. Not to me.'

'So you went to your bag, you said, sir?'

'I don't keep matches or cigarettes in my pocket. There's a zipped pocket on the bag. It's much more convenient.'

'I imagine so. How well do you know Mrs Bliss, sir?'

It was said in an even, conversational tone.

Purseglove hesitated.

'Your Sergeant didn't mention her.'

'I did, sir.'

But there was a strength in the man's eyes now.

'Is this relevant to your inquiries?'

'It is, sir. Otherwise I wouldn't have asked.'

Again there was a pause.

'I knew her quite well. She's a good mixer. A first-class stewardess.'

That was all he would say. Mabbatt stared at him, but he would not elaborate. He made no comment, though he allowed Purseglove to see his contempt.

'So you didn't see what happened in the spinney?'

Mabbatt grunted after a few moments.

Purseglove shook his head.

'I was looking down at the match. There was the wind and the rain,' said Purseglove. 'I'm sorry I can't help more than that. I went into the spinney right away, of course, once I'd got over the shock of hearing poor Tom make that awful noise.'

Mabbatt lost interest. He put a few more questions and told Purseglove he had been helpful.

Root caught himself yawning as Purseglove was thanked. When he had gone, Mabbatt glared at the picture of the spinney once more.

'He should have seen or heard something!' he growled. 'He was right against the spinney!'

Root thought of the rain on the bright leaves.

'He wouldn't be thinking about anything but golf, sir.'

46

'Golf!' sneered Mabbatt, and Root bristled. 'Committee-men! Stewardesses! Bloody red anoraks!' He scowled at the dapper representation of Purseglove. 'I hate 'em here!'

Root pushed down hard on the indignation he felt. Golf was not a pursuit to be mocked like this; Mabbatt, however, was a Superintendent. If he could find how a murderer managed to remain invisible in a small copse, and then make his murder weapon disappear into thin air, he was entitled to his opinions, however absurd.

'That scrounger should have seen something!' Mabbatt complained. 'Stupid bastard!'

Eight

'If a match fail to keep its place on the course . . ., it should allow the match following to pass.'

Margaret Hughes waved as Root left the bar. She saw his long, red-brown face crinkle into a smile. It had always been very obvious to Margaret that Root was that unmodern curiosity, a good and contented man. But what would Uncle Arthur think of Frank's attack on Bliss? She was in a state of considerable turmoil, for it was contrary to Frank Bell's nature to show aggression. Now, suddenly, he had made himself appear vicious. Margaret took his hands.

'Come on! It's late. It's nearly seven!'

'Oh. Oh yes. All right, Margaret.'

Frank looked down at the skinned knuckles of his right hand. He could not help looking across at the steward, who was being plastered up by Dr Fordham.

'I'm sorry,' he said to Margaret. 'It was just that he was so — damned crude about it all! I suppose I'm in trouble?'

'Nothing that won't blow over. Up, Frank!'

He allowed himself to be taken away.

Jack Lecky waved from the bar, where a few of the members had elected to remain and exhaust the remaining bottles of liqueurs. He was talking to Elaine Bliss, and she was smiling with more than professional enthusiasm.

'Take care!' called Lecky.

'What does he mean by that?' Frank said. 'You heard him!'

His face was that of an aggrieved child.

'Oh, Frank!' said Margaret exasperated. 'He means you've been upset and had a shock! He means look after yourself! Good-bye!' she called. 'Take care yourself!'

But Lecky was talking to Elaine Bliss again, and the couple went out to a few murmurs from the drinkers.

In the car park Frank halted.

'They think I did it, you know, Margaret. Oh, they do!' Frank Bell went on before she could interrupt: 'They think it's because of this golf-ball business. They think that Tyzack stole it and I found out. Mabbatt practically arrested me in there.'

Frank Bell was shuddering with emotion. Margaret's sympathy overflowed. She took him in her arms and held him.

'They do. And it's so crazy! But the ball was in his pocket. And then I had to go and hit that fool Bliss!'

The massive building loomed over them. They were in profound shadow as the sun hid itself behind the great soot-blackened pile. The mock-battlements of the tower high above them were menacing, jaw-like things. The bright green of the course had taken on a white, misty covering.

Three uniformed policemen crunched across the gravel just then, clearly on their way to the men's locker-rooms. There was a jolly intentness about their strides and their big red faces that made Margaret feel colder still.

'Oh, come on!' she said angrily.

Frank got into the Mini. It leapt away from the club like an angry rabbit.

'So you're an engineer?' Elaine Bliss was saying to Lecky, as her husband accepted a glass of Brontë liqueur from one of his cronies.

'Sort of,' said Lecky. 'Nothing very special. I'm a maintenance engineer.'

'Whereabouts?'

'At the tractor works. Duckworth's.'

'And I expect you're going to join the Club?'

'If I can.'

'Then we'll be seeing more of you?'

Elaine had noticed him standing on the first tee. Something about his face had particularly attracted her. He was a bit older than her, a squarely-built capable-looking man.

'You'll be seeing more of me.' Why not, he asked himself. Why not take up the suggestion in her eyes?

Bliss interrupted.

'I'll be off to lie down, then Elaine. That young hooligan should be up before the Committee,' he added. 'And prosecuted. I hope he gets prison. See what he's done to my face!'

Lecky was sympathetic.

'Have a drink before you go. There's some Green Chartreuse left. Or Blackberry Brandy.'

'It's a kind thought,' said Bliss. 'Thank you, sir.'

'I often have them,' Lecky said.

'Drinks?' asked Elaine, hooding her eyes slightly.

'Kind thoughts.'

'So do I.'

Bliss joined his friends with a glass in each hand, leaving his wife and Jack Lecky alone.

'You'll be coming to the Captain's Dance, then?' Elaine asked, after a pause during which she had assessed Lecky's sharply-handsome face. Only a year or two older than herself, she thought. I wonder if his wife keeps him happy?

'I hadn't meant to.'

'It'll be fun.'

'Then I'll be there.'

'That's if we have the do at all. You know,' she said, indicating the

50

police trailer. 'All this.'

Lecky had downed a good deal of whisky. He was in a thoughtful mood. Especially now that he had committed himself to an affair with the stewardess.

'What was he like?'

'Tom?'

'Yes.'

'Oh, he was a rare one!'

She began to giggle, but she stopped when her husband looked down the bar at her.

'He was!' she went on more quietly. 'Of course, he'd been a member years when I came, and I was a bit green in those days, but, oh! – he did make me laugh!'

'I heard he was quarrelsome.'

'He was! But like a kid! He'd be in the depths one minute and then chasing you round the bar the next! Do you know what he did when he met a woman he fancied? I bet you couldn't guess!'

Jack Lecky leaned closer to Elaine's magnificent bosom.

'What?'

She rocked with silent laughter at the memory.

'He had this photograph of himself, you see. He'd say "You'll only laugh! You'll all laugh!", and then someone would say they wanted to see it. And he'd show them a bit of the photo and say it was him when he was only a year old, and then they'd all want to see it properly!'

Lecky began to realize what had gone wrong with his own marriage when he saw the sheer delight in Elaine's eyes: he and his wife had never laughed together, never like this.

'He'd got this photograph,' he prompted.

'Yes!' And she was almost helpless, gripping the solid mahogany bar for support. At the far end Bliss called something, but she ignored him. 'It was his party trick – when they all wanted to see it, he'd say again "You'll only laugh – everyone does! And it's only me as a baby." And he'd keep his face straight and show it them – and on it – on it!!'

She shook convulsively.

'Elaine!' Bliss called thickly from his hurt lips.

'There was this baby, all naked, and he'd got a huge – well, you know – what boys have! Huge! Not *his* – not a baby's at all!'

'I'm going to lie down!' announced Bliss.

Elaine waved to him. The drinkers were helping themselves from a bottle of German liqueur. They were a solemn, dedicated crew, quite drunk, but utterly respectable.

'So why should anyone kill him?'

It sobered Elaine.

'It's awful! He wasn't really a gentleman – not like Mr Purseglove or Mr Church. But he wouldn't have hurt anyone.'

'Someone didn't like him.'

'Of course, there was his temper! I've seen him jump up and down out on the course. And him such a big man! He had terrible rages!'

Lecky saw that she was beginning to be affected by the strain of the day's events.

'They'll find the one who did it.'

Lecky heard the powerful engine of a police car. He wondered whether he should go: but to what? Television? He hadn't troubled to put up the aerial since his wife had written to say she wouldn't be joining him. Week-ends were the worst when you were single again. Houses were too big, had too much silence.

'I'd like a cup of tea,' he found himself saying.

'So would I!' said Elaine. 'I'll make one.'

Nine

'Foreign material shall not be applied to a ball . . .'

It was past eight o'clock. Root thought of his Sunday dinner, the meal he should have eaten at half-past one. It would be over-cooked and steamy, but the thought of it made his mouth water. And still there was no sign of Mabbatt releasing him.

Root concentrated on the enlarged map of the course. As he gazed at the tiny first tee, his thoughts wandered. He began to go through his shots the last time he had played. Nicely off the first with a three-wood. A spoon if you wanted to be old-fashioned. Then a six-iron to the edge of the green – a run-up with the same six-iron and a putt – no! Two putts, for the first had been pushed off-line by a heel-mark. It should have been a four. He wondered how Tyzack had felt only a few hours earlier. Tom had made a very good putt to take a birdie three.

'What did you make of that little bugger Parsons?' Mabbatt said, addressing the others for the first time in five minutes.

The Geordie sorted through the neatly-typed statements.

'Opportunity. And he had reason to want Tyzack harmed. But not enough reason. He's on a good thing with the Steel woman. She's loaded.'

'Root?' asked Mabbatt.

'Parsons isn't a killer, sir,' Root said. 'When he's in trouble, he runs.'

'What makes you say that?'

'He deserted his family. Found a young woman in Sheffield. After that he went off with her mother.'

The gaunt Geordie hid a smile.

Mabbatt was disgusted. 'When?'

'Six years ago, sir. He ran out on her too. Now he's running out on this club.'

'He isn't running – he's been sacked!'

'Half-a-dozen each way, sir. Mrs Steel's setting him up in business. A sports store.'

'If looks are anything to go by, he'll find it hard running out on her,' said Bickerdike.

'Get back to Tyzack,' Mabbatt told Strapp. 'Parsons' statement. Read it out.'

' "Tom had a terrible swing when he came to me",' Strapp began. Root nodded. It was true: terrible. ' "I tried to get him to swing slowly, but he went back like a fiddler's elbow. I think he tried other local pros for lessons, but it was no good. He should have been a middle-handicap man, off about fourteen or sixteen, but he'd got a good eye for the ball, so he was down to four. The latest handicap revision would have pulled him to three. I liked him, and I don't care if he did help to get me the push. I'd drink with him any day of the week, and I wouldn't say that about many of the bastards here." '

Mabbatt grunted, a sound very much like one of agreement.

'What did his girl-friend have to say?'

Strapp turned to Denise Steel's statement:

' "I was standing below the spinney trying to hit a leaf as Jack had told me. Jack went to get some of the plastic balls I'd been trying to hit. I heard a scream or a yell, very loud, then I tried to hit the leaf again. I couldn't see Jack at that time, because I was concentrating on trying to hit the leaf." '

'She doesn't say she saw him in the spinney, and she doesn't say she didn't,' said Mabbatt. 'According to his own statement, he was in it. What does she say about Tyzack?'

'That's all, sir,' said Sergeant Strapp.

Root fixed his eyes on the small-scale map of the course. He noticed Williamson's shabby, cloth-capped image. Mabbatt had handled him badly. Root speculated on his own preferred method of interrogation, a sort of sustained chat. But village-bobby methods were out of place; and anyway, what more could Williamson have added? There had been a certain hesitancy in his answers, yet his statement was clear enough. No, thought Root, it was better to be forthright with Williamson's kind. His hesitancy was the usual bloody-mindedness of the South Yorkshire collier faced with the familiar enemy: authority. If Williamson had seen or heard anything out of the ordinary he would have said so: reluctantly, but graphically. Root's gaze passed on, ranging over the course. He thought of Tyzack's last game of golf. All about the little spot where Tom had been killed, the Sunday morning fourballs had moved on, from first to second, second to third, and on and on, a stately and dignified procession, wheeling around the centre of the course like a great clock.

'Bliss,' said Mabbatt.

'Sir,' said Bickerdike, taking a statement from the heap.

'He was in the tent. No one else. Getting ready to serve his customers. His wife wouldn't do that?' Mabbatt inquired of Root.

'Not usually, sir. He'd want to be out in the open. His bit of fresh air for the week, if it was a fine day. He would have a beer himself if anyone bought him one.'

'He could have slipped out of the back?' offered Strapp.

Mabbatt shrugged.

'He could. Go on,' he told Bickerdike. 'Let's hear what he says.'

It would be neutral, thought Root. However much Bliss tattled in private, he would be careful to keep on the right side of the Committee.

' "Mr Tyzack was a very considerate gentleman," ' read Strapp.
' "He was generous and very amiable. I valued his custom.' "

Mabbatt made a deep grunting sound.

'Creep! And his wife having it off with the man!'

'It was his idea, sir,' Root pointed out.

Mabbatt said viciously:

'Ponce!'

Root wondered whether this was the moment to tell Mabbatt about Tyzack's fairly complicated love-life. He was beginning to feel tired and dispirited. He thought longingly of the familiar round of duties in his village. The boy Smethurst should be given a talking-to. His father thought he might be on some sort of pills. Then there was the bricks – how did they get them away? There should have been tracks in the wet mud: how could half a ton of bricks be removed without *some* trace? Hovercraft?

Root grinned slightly.

He decided to save his information for a little later. 'Bliss wouldn't have done it,' said Mabbatt.

Strapp disagreed.

'It might have been the final straw, sir. Tyzack seems to have been rather an uncouth type.'

'Like me!' chuckled Mabbatt.

No one answered.

'No!' Mabbatt said. 'That lad, what was his name – Bell. Saw him in tears not long ago. Well, Root?'

'Decent young fellow, sir. Grammar School, University. Father's a shop-keeper, newsagent's. Been engaged to Margaret Hughes since they fell over one another when their mothers were collecting the orange juice.'

'Know him well, don't you?'

'It's my job to know people in the village, sir.'

'A real village bobby, eh?'

Mabbatt was not being complimentary.

'That's right, sir,' said Root, who would have defended the title to the end.

'Violent?'

'Never, sir.'

'He was today.'

'Overwrought, sir.'

Mabbatt swung to confront the gaunt Geordie.

'Have you charged him, Sergeant?'

'Well, sir, I didn't think – '

'Try to talk Bliss out of complaining,' ordered Mabbatt, to Root's relief.

Root tried not to let his relief show. It was Margaret he wished to protect.

'What did Parsons mean?' demanded Mabbatt.

'Sir?' asked Root.

'He said good golfers used them. Looked as though he enjoyed a joke or something.'

'That, sir. Yes. Findable golf-balls. He meant that good golfers don't lose golf-balls. So good golfers always have findable golf-balls.'

Mabbatt fumbled in a wire basket and drew out the golf-ball.

'He reckons it might have been worth money. How much?'

Root tried to recall what he knew of the manufacture of golf-balls.

'The golf companies would be interested if he really has something,' he said after a few moments. 'I've no idea about figures, but golf-balls are very big business. A company might buy him out to keep it off the market altogether. But it might not be anything, sir. It's a completely unproven idea.'

'Supposing Tyzack thought it was valuable?'

'Frank would still have the patent, sir.'

Mabbatt frowned. It was like a cliff crumbling.

'Supposing he hadn't bothered to take out patent rights?'

'There's that, sir,' agreed Root. 'But it's all very speculative.'

'So's any business.'

'There could be another explanation, sir,' offered Root.

'Aye?'

Bickerdike and Strapp leaned forward.

'Tom could have put the ball in his pocket because it was a new ball. Simple theft, sir.'

But Mabbatt didn't like the idea.

'I want to know if it's worth money.'

'I could get in touch with one of the manufacturers,' Strapp offered.

Mabbatt thought about it.

'Aye,' he said.

'I'll ring first thing tomorrow, sir.'

'Good. Now. Church: what does he say?'

He swung away to look at the bright police artist's map. Root had the sensation of being left suspended on one of the aerial wires that took spoil to the slag-heaps of South Yorkshire.

'There's not much, sir,' said Strapp. 'He says, in effect, that Tyzack was a rough diamond, self-made, very reliable, and a bit of a noddy. He didn't see anything in the spinney – too busy prodding around tufts of grass to look up. Heard something, heard the bushes swished aside, but didn't bother to look around. Assumed it was Purseglove or Bell or Tyzack looking for the ball. He caught sight of the scrounger, Williamson, but didn't take any notice.'

Mabbatt put a heavy finger on a figure on the map. 'Why couldn't this bloody Purseglove have kept his eyes open!'

'It would have helped, sir,' agreed Strapp. 'Still, there was a bit of a wind blowing and he'd have had trouble lighting up. He'd not be taking notice of much else.'

Mabbatt stared with dislike at Purseglove's tiny, red figure.

'Get some beer,' he said to Root.

'Sorry, sir. None left.'

'What!'

'Bar's almost cleared out. They were on to the fancy stuff when I left. The few that were left.'

'They'll be well-oiled,' suggested Strapp delicately.

'No!' said Mabbatt. 'I can just see it in the papers – drunks, fights, golf and a murder! Oh, no! Get them home, but don't let them drive! Strapp – you see to it. Bickerdike, get me the latest on the search.'

The two sergeants left.

It struck Root that this was the moment.

'Now we've a minute, sir?' he suggested.

Mabbatt was arranging the statements of the principal witnesses.

'It's about Tyzack's domestic arrangements, sir.'

'Well?'

He would never make a golfer, thought Root. He'd be one of those utterly uncoordinated men who tried to make strength do the work of balance and contained power.

'It's general knowledge that the deceased had two households, sir.'

Mabbatt's thick upper lip drew back:

'I swear they're like bloody jack-rabbits!'

'It's a Miss Jenny Piggott. She used to be a petrol-pump attendant. Tom set her up in a bungalow.'

Root was uncomfortably aware that he had held back information. Mabbatt shook his huge head in disbelief.

'Rabbits!' he repeated. 'Bloody jack-rabbits!'

'I've got the address, sir.'

Mabbatt ignored him.

Ten

'No one should move, talk or stand close . . . when a player is . . . making a stroke.'

Root contemplated the map of the course once more as Mabbatt re-arranged the piles of paper. He seemed to be looking for something that couldn't possibly be amongst them.

Strapp was the first to return.

'All organized, sir.'

Mabbatt thumped the table.

'Here, Strapp. See if you can make yourself useful. Read these – I want Tyzack's words. What he said. Get it all fixed in your mind.'

Root knew what he was looking for. Mabbatt was attempting to do what any detective must : re-create the state of mind of the victim immediately before his killing. The theory was that anything a man said just before his death would be relevant to the death. Root was sceptical. It smacked too much of mysticism. There was a primordial belief that death touched the soul before the final meeting ; it might be true of a person dying of a lingering illness, but hardly of a vigorous man struck down by an unseen enemy whilst enjoying the misery of Sunday morning golf.

'Root,' Mabbatt said.

PC Root sprang to attention at the sharp call. He had been dreaming again.

'Sir!'

'Where would a man hide a golf-stick?'

For a moment Root was inclined to smile; he controlled his facial muscles and was glad of it.

'Almost anywhere on the course, sir. Down a rat-hole. In a drainage dyke, pushed down. Even up a tree.'

'Go on.'

'In his locker. In someone else's golf-bag. Any place in the building here. It's a huge, rambling place.'

'Aye. And he could just chuck it out into the scrub. Or he could put it in his car. But, like as not, someone would see him; and remember!'

'The pro's shop, sir,' said Root thoughtfully. It could be. There were scores of clubs of all kinds, battered relics of the Sarazen era, shiny things with names like 'Dyna-Power' and 'Supa-Play', and miscellaneous, functional clubs that had lost their shine but were still passed on from newcomer to newcomer as they were traded and re-traded for better clubs.

'Aye.'

Mabbatt did not think much of his contribution, Root saw. He'd thought of all of these, or Bickerdike had. The next stage was obvious. They'd have to go over the likely areas of the course, inch by inch, with metal-detectors.

'I'll want you at dawn,' Mabbatt said. 'We'll have the marvels of modern science out.'

Bickerdike returned.

'Nothing, sir.' he reported. 'The light isn't good. We've almost completed the house too, the parts of it that are getatable.'

Mabbatt scowled.

'That's bloody marvellous. It is. No direct witness. No direct evidence. No weapon. No one in custody. And everyone heard the man being killed!'

The Geordie wanted to go home too:

'We've got most of the statements we want, sir. The scroungers. One of the maids who help in the kitchen. And the two youths who work for Parsons. They've all been packed off home.'

Mabbatt's scowl deepened.

'I hate these things! Look at it!'

He pointed to the bright map of the spinney.

'It's all there! We should have had him inside by now! It's mid-morning, and the place is crowded – the copse is full of people, they're crawling all over it like wood lice, and no one saw a single sodding thing!'

Root began to appreciate the problems of a senior officer. He could find no sympathy at all for Mabbatt.

'So we have to graft, sir,' said Bickerdike.

It was clear that he looked forward to the prospect.

'Aye! We take Tyzack's life apart!'

'Go through those with Strapp,' ordered Mabbatt, pointing to the statements. 'Come on,' he said to Root.

'You come with me. We'll have a look at the place.'

The mansion was superb. Whoever had designed the staircase, for instance, had had an eye for the majestic. It was wide – scuffed now, of course – and ornate. The marble balustrades curved away gracefully, ending in representations of classical ladies. Dryads? wondered Root. Nymphs? Church was always complaining that visitors put their hats on the stone curls. It spoiled the tone of the place, he said.

'Listen,' commanded Mabbatt. 'You try to carry on as normal. You play golf as you normally do. More, if you can. Watch. Think. Go in the bar. If there's anything special coming off, you attend. Got it?'

'Sir.'

Would there be expenses? And overtime pay? Root was not an acquisitive man, but, he told himself, he owed it to his Yorkshire blood not to turn an honest penny away.

62

'And *listen*! That's your job!'

'There's this, sir,' said Root.

He indicated the notice-board.

There was the ornate poster: *Club Dance. The Annual Captain's Dance.*

'Next Saturday?'

'Yes, sir.'

'You'd go?'

'It's our one big event of the year, sir, Mrs Root and me.'

'Dinner jacket!' exclaimed Mabbatt, reading the notice through. 'A village bobby in a dinner jacket!'

Root was not offended.

'Sir.'

'You'll be wanting expenses next!'

'Yes, sir,' said Root definitely.

Mabbatt's face creased into what passed for a smile.

'Aye.'

A plainclothes officer who was a stranger to Root came across.

'Nothing at all, sir,' he said. 'We could set up lights.' He was unenthusiastic about the idea.

'Send them home,' said Mabbatt. 'Bickerdike will talk to them first.'

'We found a few more golf-balls, sir.'

Root felt fingers of greed clutching at his golfer's soul.

'Let Bickerdike have them.'

'Parsons was asking when he could have his club back. The one that's identical with the missing iron.'

'I'll talk to him tomorrow.'

'Sir.'

And that was all, thought Root.

Darkness was falling fast as the afterglow set up a lurid redness amongst the vast elms. The architect had been a man of some imagination. He had left the three or four hundred-year-old elms as a back-cloth to the thrusting arrogance of the four great towers. The trees were in full leaf now, canopies of greenery made things of mystery by the vivid red glow of the sun's last beams. Or so Root thought. He had a taste for the mid-Victorian novel, and such phrases as 'canopies of greenery' came quite naturally to him amongst the romantic surroundings of what had been Wolvers Park. It was, of course, frightful that such places had been built on the sweat of skinny children hauling on coal-tubs beneath the pretty walks of the Park : but the Hall was a here and now, and he, Root, could stroll where once his kind would have not dared set foot. And he could look at the marvellous outline of the Hall against the theatrical sunset : great swathes of cloud, red and cream and white ; black towers and the tracery of elms ; the redness of the sun and the stark blackness of Wolvers Hall.

'Must have cost a fortune,' said Mabbatt.

'There's talk of pulling it down, sir,' said Root. 'But that would cost a fortune too.'

Mabbatt regarded the impressive bulk of the Hall.

'I'd put a bomb under it.'

Root wanted to say 'I expect you would', but he didn't. Mabbatt was a man without imagination.

'Let's get at those statements again,' ordered Mabbatt. 'Strapp and Bickerdike have had long enough.'

The two sergeants were showing signs of fatigue.

Strapp's rosy cheeks were redder than usual ; Bickerdike's gaunt and unhealthy-looking face was cadeverous : but they could face Mabbatt.

'Well ?' he asked.

Strapp began :

'They weren't a talkative lot, sir, but we've got a complete schedule of all Tyzack said from the moment he reached the course to the time of his death. There are bits from Parsons, from one of the assistant professionals, from two golfers who saw him in the locker-rooms – that's where they change for golf, sir – and then from his partners. So far as we can trace, he didn't talk to anyone else that morning, though we can check on the complete list of statements by tomorrow night.'

'Right.'

'He arrived at the course at eight-fifty-five in a blue Rover 2000. He'd got his clubs in the back of the car, which was usual for him.'

'He came alone?'

'Yes, sir.'

'That usual?'

'Yes, sir.'

Root could see him now. Burly Tom Tyzack blitzing up the road from Wickinglow thinking of the prize money for the best score: Tom was a bad loser, and an overbearing winner. Cockahoop when ahead, he was in black despair if the game went against him.

There wasn't much to go on. He had bought two new golf-balls. That was quite usual. The youth who had served him couldn't remember anything apart from Tyzack saying 'Two of those', passing the money across and shouting 'You randy bugger!' to Parsons.

Parsons confirmed the words.

Apparently Tom had passed the same kind of raucous comment to two casual acquaintances in the lower locker-room, and then he had gone upstairs to his own locker. Purseglove was already changed and out at the first tee by this time. Church was late, arriving as Tyzack laced up his black-and-white golf shoes. But Frank Bell had talked to Tyzack for a minute or two.

' "Tom wasn't in a specially good humour, but he wasn't what you'd call miserable",' read Strapp. ' "He said it was a pity about Parsons having to go, then he asked me if I was going for a drink after the game. I said I might if we finished early. Then he asked me if the glass technologist had come up with anything." '

'That's the business about the findable golf-ball – Bell's invention, sir,' put in Bickerdike. 'Bell hadn't made any secret of it. He'd got a friend at Kenyon's in one of the research departments. This friend was building up a special kind of paint that made a golf-ball show up better. Tyzack would have known about this two or three months before, when Bell first talked of it.'

'Aye.'

Root swayed. It had been a long day, and the night before had been long too. It couldn't be Frank? Not *Frank*! It was too far-fetched.

Strapp looked at Mabbatt who nodded for him to continue.

' "I said he had and that I'd got half-a-dozen balls coated. He didn't say much then. Phil Church passed us as we left for the tee. Phil said he'd hurry. He'd come ready to play and it was only a matter of him getting his shoes on. Tom said Phil was always like that – rushing around to catch his tail." '

'Was he?' demanded Mabbatt.

Root realized that the question was for him.

'Yes, sir. He's always in a hurry.'

It was all so very ordinary. The four men had arrived at the clubhouse. They had exchanged greetings in the usual way; apart from the conversation between Bell and Tyzack, there was nothing that could not have been said by any one of the seventy or so competitors in the Medal Round. Like most of the golfers, they had arranged a side-stake on the round.

'There isn't much on the course, either, sir,' said Strapp. 'Sergeant Bickerdike did that.'

There wasn't. Root listened to the badinage of the golf course. The mixture was familiar. 'It weren't bad,' Tyzack had admitted of his birdie three at the first. He had taken the honour and driven off at the second; he hooked miserably, his ball ending on the adjoining fairway. He had said something to Purseglove, who then played a much worse shot. You won't get this one – my mate'll do you,' he told Purseglove. And Church had put his ball safely down the middle. However, Frank had played well to halve with Tyzack and Church on fives. There had been some tension at the third, when Tyzack had accused Frank Bell of deliberately placing his shadow across the line of his putt. 'That's against rules!' Tyzack had burst out. 'You might as well bring a bloody brass band as well! But it won't put me off,' he had added. It had, and he missed the putt.

He had rowed with Purseglove briefly on the fourth; and he had told his own partner, Phil Church, to stuff himself when Phil had asked him to replace a divot. But none of these things were out of the ordinary or out of character. Tyzack had remained in a more or less

66

ill-humoured state until the seventh, when he had driven a magnificent tee-shot almost three hundred yards straight down the fairway. His remark to his opponents, Bell and Purseglove, after making the fine tee-shot on the seventh: 'Makes your drives look like long putts, doesn't it?' was the kind of arrogant boastfulness that everyone accepted – expected – from Tom Tyzack. He was ebulliently hateful when playing well. 'We'll have your money!' he boasted. 'You'll get nowt!'

Root could not help grinning at the memory of Tyzack's huge glee. He had often played with the big, ungainly man. Whatever his faults, he had been a vital figure at Wolvers. He would be missed. But not by one person.

'Nothing!' grunted Mabbatt. 'Just that bloody game!'

Root spoke, more out of boredom than anything else:

'Golf's like that, sir. You just don't think of anything else while you're playing.'

Mabbatt turned the vast head towards him.

'You play this week, Root! You play, and you think of other things. Think of this!' he growled, pounding the desk. 'Think of it all the time!'

'Sir.'

Bickerdike took a message from a uniformed constable. The gaunt Geordie stood up.

'The papers, sir. Reporters.'

Root's natural good sense prevented him from openly yawning. It was ten past ten, and he had not had more than five hours sleep in the past thirty-six hours. How long would Mabbatt keep him? He was looking forward to seeing his wife again. His dinner would be in the oven, soggy and delicious. Ursula would have stoked the kitchen boiler to make sure he could have a hot bath. Tonight there was no need for a patrol. The local sneak-thief who was accumulating car tools from unlocked garages was not his concern; nor was the thief who could magically transport heavy house-bricks without leaving a trace.

'I'll see them,' said Mabbatt. 'In the bar.'

Root blinked.

'Go to bed,' Mabbatt told him. 'Get a night's sleep.'

'Thank you, sir.'

Root's long face split into a brilliant smile. He was going home. Then he remembered the tears on the face of Margaret Hughes. Tyzack's death was going to bring changes to a number of lives.

'Well, get off,' said Sergeant Strapp. 'We'll be here half the night.'

'Good night.'

Strapp stopped him.

'Do you think they'll be taking on new members?'

'Why?'

'I'm thinking of putting in an application here.'

'Doubtful. Good night.

Strapp burrowed into the statements again.

Eleven

'In a three-ball match, each player is playing two distinct matches.'

The bus was full of women going to the peanuts factory and men returning from the night-shift at one of the smaller collieries. The women were tired, pale-faced and overweight, the miners were scrupulously clean, apart from the black rims to their eyes. Root was not in uniform but he felt out of place amongst the workpeople. It was almost like going on holiday, taking the bus to Wolvers.

Mabbatt was already at the course. He wasn't sure about Root. Root had a good record, but he didn't seem to have any sort of go about him. Still police-constable at forty. What was wrong with him? Mabbatt put his mind to the investigation.

Root walked up the long drive, conscious of the activity already in progress around the clubhouse. He grinned as he caught sight of a face in a thick patch of trees: an early-morning ball-scavenger. He would soon be chased away by the Task Force guards. Whoever he was, the scrounger had the trick of merging into the background which was the sign of all Wolvers' successful gleaners. The face vanished, leaving Root with an awareness of cunning and great stupidity.

Jack Parsons was up early too. He called across to Mabbatt:

'Finished with my wedge? I don't want it marked. It's one of a set.'

Mabbatt felt dislike raising the short hairs on the back of his bull's neck. Parsons' cheeky, pugnacious face showed disrespect and over-confidence.

'I'd like to keep it for a day or two. We're looking for the murder weapon again this morning. I'd appreciate your co-operation.'

'As long as they don't start pitching up with it. Found your murderer yet?'

'No, sir,' said Mabbatt in a dead voice. 'But I will.'

Parsons was undismayed.

'It's no good looking at me! Why kill the cash customers!'

'So Mr Tyzack was a good customer of yours, sir?'

Parsons shook his head.

'Tom always wanted a discount. I couldn't compete with the discount stores. He only bought the odd ball or two. But he wasn't a bad old bastard.'

Parsons walked away. He reappeared carrying a heavy bag of glittering and obviously costly golf-clubs. He winked at Strapp; then he crossed the lawn and set up a ball on the first tee.

He smacked it long and hard straight down the still-misty fairway in a sweet parabola until it was a tiny ghost-dot in the whiteness. Strapp blinked in admiration, but Parsons was not satisfied. He shook his head, looked down at his right wrist and then slowly rolled the club in his big hands. Mabbatt watched the whole performance.

Parsons teed up another ball; he executed a perfect shoulder turn, began to bring the club through, and halted it six inches from the ball. He waggled his wrists once more.

At least a dozen policemen were watching by this time, as well as one of Parsons' young assistants. It was obvious that here was an expert setting about his profession with skill and dedication. Parsons was stocky and muscular, but so were scores of the members at Wolvers; many were as athletic as Parsons, and bigger. Yet the little pro could explode into and through the space containing the few ounces of materials that made up the golf ball with such dynamic energy that the ball screamed away as if driven by gunpowder.

Parsons swung.

The ball thrummed through the air, out across the hill-side and away into the mist until it pitched into a smoky distant corridor.

'Over three hundred yards,' said Strapp.

Parsons grinned over his shoulder.

'Hello, Arthur!' he called, seeing Root. 'Come to have a knock?'

Root was still in a state of wonder at the display of power. 'Sorry,' he said, after a moment. 'Afraid I'm on duty, Jack.'

Parsons waved and left to begin his morning round. He was a busy professional and something of a trophy-hunter. It was good for trade to mop up the prizes in the locality; and there were always women at the tournaments. But his playing days were numbered: Denise Steel would keep him out of the way of the golfing women of Yorkshire.

'Cocky little bugger,' said Mabbatt.

'Would you like some tea?' called Elaine Bliss.

She was looking down at them from the steward's flat, which overlooked the first half of the course. She was astonishingly attractive. Strapp licked his lips. Mabbatt turned to face her.

'No.'

'I just thought, seeing as you were all up so early?'

Mabbatt ignored her. She shrugged her plump shoulders and closed the window. Root thought Mabbatt was wrong to be offensive. It was bad public relations, bad police procedure, and anyway he could have done with a cup of tea.

Elaine Bliss recognized the cause of Mabbatt's dislike. He was sex-starved. He fancied her, and he couldn't have her. Like some of the more unpleasant members at Wolvers, he affected to despise the men who had an opportunity to enjoy her. She dressed slowly. Her husband was still in bed; he would probably stay there until lunch-time, when a few of the local businessmen might bring in customers for a steak, a drink, and a game of billiards. Bliss would want to be on hand to give his version of the events of Sunday.

She thought of Jack Lecky. He had told her about his failed

marriage. Men usually talked about their wives soon after they had made love to a new woman. Jack wanted to know why his wife had left him; he couldn't see that some women would leave any man. Elaine allowed herself to dwell on the love-making that had taken place in one of the more remote rooms at Wolvers Hall. She had taken Jack to one of the tower apartments. It was a strange room, circular, unlighted and unheated. There was no furniture. The original paintings on the ceiling and walls – woodland scenes, with large bare ladies, and men in feathered hats – could just be seen in the light filtering through narrow, thin windows.

She could have taken him to her own apartment, for Charlie Bliss would be asleep. But Jack was different from the others. Elaine had always had a romantic attachment to the tower-room; it was fitting that they should begin the liaison there. And it had been delicious. The gay, ghostly, bleak room was dusty and eerie. The pools of moonlight on the faded flowers and smiling ladies provided just that air of elegant decadence that Elaine loved to read about in the novels of Miss Heyer. It was like being seventeen again and meeting one of the boys from the grammar school out in the woods beyond the pit marshalling-yard. When an owl hooted just outside the battlements, Elaine had giggled with ecstasy.

'Jack, oh, Jack!' she said, clinging to him. 'Why didn't you come along before! It's never been like this, never!'

And, for want of anything else to say, she told him about the Committee.

'*I* didn't want to start it! It was his idea! I mean, they're old – much older than me. Not as old as they might be, but Mr Church must be well into his fifties.'

She paused, for she knew that it was inexcusable to discuss still-current affairs with a new lover.

'And Tom Tyzack?'

Elaine gurgled. She thought of Tom's big, dead shrouded figure being taken to the ambulance. She remembered his big-nosed Mr Punch face. She clung to Jack again.

'Poor Tom! It wasn't like being with a man – if you know what I mean!'

Lecky patted her head.

He thought he knew. His own wife was a bright, nervous woman, constantly seeking reassurance from what she imagined were mature men and women.

'He were a joke, Tom! Always making you laugh! And he wasn't mean with me – he always brought me something. Once it were a watch. A good one. Once he even brought me a brace of pheasants – I didn't know what to do with them! Charlie had to pluck and clean them, then we had them at night. And that were last year! He didn't bother again when he'd got that girl up at Thurlby.'

'Forget it,' said Jack.

'I can't!'

But she tried.

Now, annoyed at being ignored by Mabbatt, she bustled about the apartment with vacuum cleaner and dusting cloths. She was a vigorous woman who enjoyed all forms of physical activity. Even pushing the cleaner around the big rooms was a pleasure; Bliss called for quietness after a while, but she laughed at him.

'You get up, Charlie! It'll do you good to be out of bed early for once.'

'Bring me some tea, love!'

Elaine yelled a mild obscenity at him, but she made his tea. She had long since learned that the basis of a successful married life was to satisfy the small, immediate needs of a partner.

'I bet they won't cancel the Captains,' Bliss complained. He would avoid, if he could, the added burden of catering for the entire membership of the club and their guests on the day of the annual Captain's Invitation Match and Dance.

'I should hope not!' said his wife.

'It's not right. They should show respect.'

'Tom wouldn't mind.'

Bliss put on a mournful expression.

'Mr Tyzack isn't here to mind.'

'Oh, Charlie, you're a right creep! You are!'

'He's clever, you know,' said Bliss. He had that alert, knowing air which Elaine had once thought attractively superior.

'Who is ?'

'Him that did it.'

'He's not clever ! Anyone that does a murder isn't clever – he's bound to be caught !'

Bliss smiled secretively.

'Oh, no, Oh, no, Elaine. Not if he's clever enough.'

She knew that Charlie Bliss was trying a quite usual trick, that of appearing to know more than he really did. Sly, clever Charlie !

Elaine was becoming bored. She wondered if Lecky would call in during the week or whether she would have to wait till the night of the Dance to see him again. For a moment she allowed herself to think of him as the only man she need live with. It was an inviting prospect. Charlie still looked sly and knowing. *Charlie ?*

'You could have done it,' she said, surprising herself.

'Me ! I was in the tent ! Superintendent Mabbatt knows that ! He told me I was in the clear. He wants me to help with his investigation – and I can, you know !'

'You know bugger all !' Elaine flashed at him, angry at Bliss's air of triumphant secrecy.

'I suppose you do – you and your precious Committee-men !'

Elaine got to her feet. She could have hit him. He watched her, knowing that she could be dangerous when roused; he was a cowardly man. He had a pillow ready to catch her blow. She saw it and laughed, still angry :

'It were your idea ! You said be nice to them, and you knew just what you was doing, Charlie Bliss ! *And* you had your own fancy piece, that one that used to do the washing up ! *And* you said it didn't matter, them being gentlemen. You don't know bugger all, Charlie ! And you're a lying lazy sod ! And there's something you don't know and I'll tell you ! Mr Tyzack would have outed you long ago but for me ! He'd have set me up years ago. Just like that girl at Thurlby !'

Bliss began to raise himself from the bed, but his wife's furious gesture stopped him. She had a tin of furniture polish in her hand, and the edges looked sharp. He warned himself to be careful.

'It's got to stop !' he said. 'It has. All this messing about with the members – you shouldn't be doing it, Elaine! I mean, I am your husband!'

'Husband!'

'Yes! And another thing – I saw you with that new member.'

'He's not a member!'

'Well, whoever he is!'

'I'll please myself, Charlie Bliss!'

'You won't!'

'I bloody well will!'

'They can hear us out there!'

'Let them!'

'They'll all hear – suppose Mr Church has called in!'

'I don't care!'

'Let me drink my tea in peace, love! My head's bursting where that lad hit me. It isn't right! He's bigger than me. And he's supposed to be a gentleman.'

Elaine's anger evaporated at once. She knew that she was the stronger of the two, and also that she had lived for too long with Bliss's cunning, devious personality to be able to disentangle herself from him.

'Yes. Drink your tea, Charlie. It'll get cold.'

Twelve

'The side shall be penalized for a violation . . . by either partner.'

Root examined the metal-detector. The constable who had been trained in its use explained the principles of the machine. It was simple enough to operate.

They were to check the spinney, an area of about two thousand square yards. Under the direction of the expert, white tape was put down to mark off the search area into manageable tracts. It was a dull job, relieved at times by the discovery of irrelevant bits of lost or discarded metal. There was one moment of excitement, however. Numerous metal buttons, metal-tipped pencils, beer cans, bottle-tops, and nameless rusting things had been found; even a couple of cigarette lighters, and one cigar case, had been turned up, as well as coins to a surprisingly large value. Then, in the soft, loamy soil, the machine had ferreted out án object of some size. Carefully, Root pushed away the leaves, the thick grass, and the black earth. It was a golf-club. Or part of one.

'That's it!' said the expert.

He tapped his machine with pride.

Root was elated. Heart pounding, he moved enough of the debris away to make out the shape of the metal. He willed the metal shape to take on a brighter hue. But it wouldn't.

'It's an old one,' he said. 'It's been there years!'

It was the head of someone's putter. Its ancient surface was pitted.

'Then how did it get there?'

'Someone lost it,' said Root. 'There's a bit of wood left in the socket. That makes it over thirty years old. They stopped using wooden shafts before the war.'

The search went on throughout the morning. There was an unspoken feeling amongst the slow-moving teams of searchers that they would not find the missing wedge. Yet the painstaking search proceeded with the same thoroughness as before. Root wished he could have had that early morning cup of tea. When refreshments were brought, it turned out to be canteen coffee.

Mabbatt drank his morning coffee from delicate porcelain. Mrs Tyzack had made it. She was an uncommunicative woman who had found it difficult to understand that her Tom wasn't going to pound into the large house full of whisky and boasting of his golf shots. Of course she knew that he was dead. The solicitor from Sheffield was here, and so were the police. She made a lengthy business of arranging biscuits and paper lace doileys. She hadn't loved Tom Tyzack. He had not been a lovable man. But she would miss him. Mabbatt waited.

'I haven't any fresh cream, sir, but I could open a tin.'

'Please don't trouble, Mrs Tyzack.'

'Is tinned all right?'

'Thanks.'

'I could get hot milk, sir.'

A bloody peasant, thought Mabbatt.

Tyzack's widow was a dowdy, plumpish woman of about fifty, still pretty in a plastic-doll way. You could see five hundred of them streaming into the bingo halls. He was wasting his time with her. The solicitor was a different matter altogether.

He was a florid young man with expensive clothes and gold appurtenances − heavy gold watch, bossed gold cuff-links, thick gold ring on the third finger of the left hand; his eyes expressed deferential regret when he looked at the widow, professional caution when they turned to Mabbatt and Strapp.

Mabbatt's Assistant Chief Constable knew of the young lawyer. They had talked about Tyzack's death that morning when Mabbatt's handling of the case had been subjected to a close and searching analysis.

'*Very* bright young man indeed, Mabbatt. Wish I could get one like him. You got your man yet?'

That was all that any superior would want to know, Mabbatt thought.

'I'm not speculating at this stage, sir.'

'You should! Mabbatt, you don't give yourself enough rein − use your imagination more man!'

'Young Bell could be the one.'

'The one with the findable golf-ball?'

'Yes, sir.'

'It's not for me to criticize your thinking, but he doesn't strike me as a good candidate.'

Mabbatt made a non-committal reply.

'You're sure it's one of these?' the Assistant Chief asked, when he had read the statements Mabbatt passed him.

'It has to be, sir. They're the only ones who were in the spinney at the time of the murder.'

'And the chap who was searching for golf-balls?'

'Williamson, sir.'

'According to your report, he couldn't swing a golf-club?'

'I'm making sure, sir. He'll see a police surgeon. But he's not high on my list.'

'And Bell is?'

'I'm pursuing more than one line of inquiry, sir. Tyzack was a warm man.'

'Met him once or twice myself. And his solicitor. Robinson. With Callen and Dolman in Sheffield. In fact, he is Callen and Dolman. Handle him carefully, that's my advice! You sure you can manage this inquiry? I'm asking Detective Chief Superintendent Blore to keep an eye on things so much as he can. Can you cope?'

Mabbatt did not quite conceal his distaste for the question.

'If I need help, sir, I'll ask at once.'

'Be sure you do.'

'Does that complete your inquiries here?' the solicitor wanted to know.

'I'd like to put a few questions to Mrs Tyzack.'

'I'm sure I don't know anything!'

Robinson sat his client's widow down.

'It's regrettable, Mrs Tyzack,' he said. 'We all know how you feel – this is a very sad occasion for all of us. But the police have their job to do. I promise they won't be here long, and that I'll stay in case you need me.'

Mabbatt did not argue.

'Yes, Mrs Tyzack,' he said. 'I don't want to distress you, but we have our duty. Someone struck your husband down, and it's my job to bring the murderer to justice.'

The woman looked at him with wide, shocked eyes.

'The Superintendent will be brief,' promised Robinson.

Mabbatt scowled, but the solicitor met his gaze with humorous confidence. He was a young man on the way up, and he knew it.

'We think your husband left home at about a quarter to nine yesterday, Mrs Tyzack. Is that correct?'

'Oh, yes. He was in a hurry.'

'So he was late?'

'He always were on a Sunday. I had his breakfast ready just after eight, then I had to make fresh tea when he came down at half-past, but he wouldn't have it. It were his last cup of tea, and he didn't drink it!'

She was shocked at the waste.

'Can you tell me if there was anything he said that struck you as

79

out of the ordinary, Mrs Tyzack?'

'Only that he were going to be late! And I knew what that meant!'

Robinson co-operated.

'Be frank, Mrs Tyzack! We have to help the police, however painful it might be. It's your duty, Mrs Tyzack.'

Mrs Tyzack was bitterly angry and obviously distressed:

'He were always late on a Sunday! He always had me up long before him to get his breakfast. Then there were his socks. A thick pair to play his golf in, and a spare pair for after, when he got changed and had his drink. Oh, he were clean, were Tom! Always very clean! And he drove too fast – that new car of his frightened me, and he did say he might change it. But he didn't!'

'Did anybody telephone him in the morning?'

'On Sunday?'

She hesitated.

'No! She never rang the house! She knew he'd be going there – oh, he were daft, Tom! Why should they want to kill him?'

'Who, Mrs Tyzack?' asked Mabbatt.

'Who?' she repeated stupidly. 'Who what?'

'The Superintendent thought you might have some idea about the identity of the murderer,' said Robinson. 'Have you, Mrs Tyzack?'

Mabbatt nodded. This was co-operation.

The woman stared from face to face.

'Me?'

Mabbatt knew the look. It was the face of the industrial poor of South Yorkshire confronted by a police inquiry. In it was a mixture of fear, resentment and guilt. Mrs Tyzack would be searching her memories for forgotten offences. She wouldn't accept the question at face value, because she couldn't.

'I don't think Mrs Tyzack can help you any more,' said Robinson. Quietly but with considerable firmness he added: 'I think she's too distressed to answer any more questions.'

Mabbatt ignored him.

'Mrs Tyzack,' he said to the woman: 'I'm sorry to have to press this, but I must ask you. Who stood to profit by your husband's death?'

'No,' said Robinson. But Mrs Tyzack had already begun her answer.

'Her!' she said loudly. There was no bewilderment at all in her face now. 'Her as lives at Thurlby! My Tom wouldn't have kept her for much longer – I know my Tom! He'd have put her back in her place – yes! Back on forecourt o't' garage! Likes of her, living up there! She's to get money, she is!'

'Is this true?' Mabbatt asked Robinson.

The solicitor considered his cuff-links. He turned to the panting, agitated woman.

'In the interests of justice, I have to give the police the information they need to carry out this inquiry, Mrs Tyzack. It isn't necessary for us to discuss this in front of you. Could we go into the study?'

'No! I'll go, sir! You stay in t'best room! 'You'll not want to be disturbed. Shall I get more coffee?'

It was left to Strapp to make it easy for the widow.

'I could do with some more coffee, Mrs Tyzack.'

'Yes – yes, I'll get it. It'll have to be a tin. Tom liked tinned cream best.'

She went out reminding herself to refill the sugar bowl.

Thirteen

'... a player may have the line of play indicated to him by anyone
...'

'Right,' Mabbatt said. 'Who gets his money?'

Robinson's tactful air was gone.

'You'll have to be more considerate with my client, Superintendent,' he said. 'She's a nervous and very retiring woman. Please
remember that she is in a distressed state.'

'We have a job to do, sir. No point in pretending it's a picnic. But
I'll try to go easy.'

He thought he concealed his feelings admirably.

'Very well.'

'I'd be glad of what assistance you can give, sir. My Assistant
Chief Constable said you'd co-operate.'

'I spoke to him just before you arrived.'

'Yes, sir.'

It wasn't fair. But of course they never were, the smooth

treacherous sods at the top. They had this network of self-sufficient superiority; they made the rules for themselves.

'Now, Superintendent, how can I help you?'

'I want to know who would profit from Mr Tyzack's death, sir. Who gets his money?'

'Very well, I can tell you that. The chief beneficiary is Mrs Tyzack. She inherits the bulk of Mr Tyzack's business properties and ventures. There are sums of money set aside to provide for his mother. Then there's a legacy, to a Miss Piggott.'

He waited. His sense of the dramatic overrode his easy, contained attitude.

'The mistress,' said Mabbatt.

'The mistress. She, Superintendent, inherits the maggot farm.'

'Maggot farm!'

'Exactly.'

Mabbatt shook his head wonderingly. Strapp saw that he was holding himself well in check.

'Can you tell me the approximate value of the legacy to Miss Piggott?' asked Mabbatt.

Robinson hesitated.

'Ten thousand. Perhaps a bit more. It's a profitable concern. Gross profits run at about four thousand. As a going concern the value may be fifteen thousand.'

Strapp felt rather pleased. He could understand Mrs Tyzack's annoyance; nevertheless the thought of a mistress abandoned penniless in middle age was unattractive.

'So Mr Tyzack settled the maggot farm on her when he made the will?'

'No. It was a recent acquisition. Before that he had intended that she should have the house and a small tobacconist's business. The maggot farm was bought only six months ago.'

'And he settled it on her immediately?'

'Three months ago.'

Mabbatt nodded his ponderous head.

Maggot farm. Maggots. He had used them as a boy. Fat things that you slipped onto a hook and trailed in the sour waters of the

Don. Sometimes you gave the fish a treat and chucked a handful out. Maggots. Maggot farms had the worst stench of all. It was the sweet, sick stench of the grave. The maggots lived on meat the slaughter-houses wouldn't pass: big, fat flies, selected for their size and breeding capacity, were kept to impregnate the stinking meat with larvae. Mabbatt could still remember the whiff of corruption as he opened the Sunday maggot tin.

'It's a funny sort of bequest.'

Robinson shrugged. 'Mr Tyzack was a man of humours. On this occasion, he didn't discuss his motives with me.'

'Was he likely to change his mind?'

'About Miss Piggott's bequest?'

'Yes, sir.'

Robinson smiled again.

'You're barking up the wrong tree.

All respect to the dead and all that, but Mr Tyzack knew his mind about the lady. There's no telling what he might have decided in future years, but at the time of his death he was quite satisfied with Miss Piggott's performance.'

'Can you tell me anything about the woman's style of life, sir?'

'I met the lady once, Superintendent. She was, to me, the close friend of a client. I know nothing of her circle of acquaintances, nor do I wish to comment on the propriety of her way of life. What else can I do to be of help?'

Robinson had anticipated Mabbatt's hostile questions and made them superfluous.

'I'd like to have an outline of Mr Tyzack's holdings and properties, if you don't mind, sir.'

'Certainly.'

Robinson was brisk and brief. Tyzack was a wealthy man. He owned a chain of petrol stations, amongst them two large garages. He had supermarkets in three towns. Parcels of land, suitable for house-building when he could get the necessary licences, were numbered by the dozen. There were sixteen small shops, each with a manager. The shares he owned in national and international companies were chosen on a growth basis. Mabbatt had not heard the

84

names of a good many of them.

'I'd assess his personal fortune in the hundreds of thousands,' finished Robinson. 'Mr Tyzack was an exceedingly shrewd man. During the past three years, he made a number of excellent investments. He pretty well doubled his fortune in that period.'

Mabbatt noticed the tone of satisfaction and was glad of it. The clever buggers couldn't help congratulating themselves; it showed they had a weakness.

'Had he any enemies known to you, Mr Robinson?'

Robinson played with his massy gold cuff-links.

'Two or three husbands. Some incompetents he bought out. Competitors. I've heard him say there's quite a few local people who'd cheerfully dance on his grave. But you could say that about any person in a position of wealth or authority, couldn't you, Superintendent?'

Mabbatt persevered:

'I'd appreciate any help you can give, sir.'

'No names,' Robinson said. 'I'll give you details of the financial transactions, and then you can decide for yourself who you'll interview. I'm not committing myself to a personal opinion, no matter what you say. It's not my province to do your speculating for you.'

Mrs Tyzack returned with more coffee.

'I've got your coffee, sir,' she told Mabbatt.

Robinson stared at him until he thanked her.

He left as soon as he could. In the car, he growled bitterly to Strapp for some miles on the way to Tyzack's other household. The sergeant bore it with patience; he didn't approve of Mabbatt being taken down a peg, but he wouldn't have missed it.

Fourteen

'The player is not obliged to state the reason for which he plays . . .'

At the clubhouse, Elaine Bliss was in a state of rapture. Jack Lecky had rung her to ask how she felt and to tell her that he loved her. He apologized for taking advantage of her; they had both been affected by the day's frightening happenings. He shouldn't have approached her in so direct a manner: and he would see her on the night of the Captain's Dance.

'In the painted tower?' she asked him.

'Yes. I'd like that.'

'You don't think it's daft, me wanting to go up there?'

'It isn't daft. It's a beautiful thought. And you're not sorry?'

'Me, love! No! I can get away when they're all drunk, round about twelve. There'll be the speeches and the dances, and then I can leave the bar to one of the maids. Say twelve o'clock, midnight?'

'We're acting like a pair of kids.'

'That's what I feel like, Jack. Like a kid!'

'We shouldn't have been together – made love – not when the man was lying murdered.'

'He wouldn't have minded. Tom wasn't one to be dog in manger, not Tom!'

She looked out of the window when Jack rang off. There was Arthur Root standing on the ninth tee. She waved to him, but he didn't see her. Her husband decided to get up, so she set about making his breakfast.

Already that morning more than two acres of the course had been screened. Every so often the machine pinged excitedly. It whined across the undulating parkland, revealing miscellaneous trash of the past. Brooches, metal trouser buttons, two rounds of .303 ammunition that caused something of a stir, fountain pens, groundsmen's tools, wire, pipes, coins, cigarette lighters, as well as the rusting bits of metal that might have been anything at all. No wedge, of course.

There was an element of doggedness about the search. It was becoming more and more clear that the case would not be cleared up by a stroke of fortune. The wedge had gone: no doubt of it now. But someone had to have taken it! Who? Obviously the murderer, but how? Root looked back at the spinney. He thought of the circle of shocked, intent faces. Many of the golfers still carried an iron or a putter. But all had been accounted for : the wedge had not been taken by one of them. It had disappeared at some time before they arrived, They needed a bit of luck, thought Root.

Of course there was always the chance of a psychological crack-up. The murderer might reveal himself through some change in his living habits. He might even come up with a confession. Mabbatt would have that particular angle sewn up. There would be a certain amount of discreet surveillance through the network of beat bobbies. But Root didn't think either the questioning or the watching would do much good.

It was a hard one. He felt it in his policeman's bones. It would be nasty. They weren't going to get that bit of luck.

Tyzack's mistress lived only a few minutes' drive from the Tyzack home. She was a well-made woman of about thirty-five. Strapp liked her at once. She had the uncomplicated attractiveness of a small-town Yorkshire girl who had been around but was basically still one with the people she belonged to.

Her eyes were probably her best feature. They were wide-set and of a blue that was almost green. Strapp was reminded of the subtle shifts of the light on the sea off a beach near Newquay. One day the sea would be innocuously blue, and the next, a strange indeterminate blue-green. She smiled at Strapp.

Mabbatt did not speak for some time.

Miss Piggott had furnished the bungalow with a view to comfort. Chintz-covered armchairs of great solidity; Axminster rugs on parquet; a cluster of brasses over the chimney-piece; these were the essential features of the room. Strapp liked it. His own wife would have turned up her nose at almost everything in it. But it suited the well-proportioned Jenny Piggott. It was her life-style, as the clever magazines said. Something disturbed him until he saw her against the comfortable, unfashionable room. He knew what it was now.

Jenny Piggott was another Mrs Tyzack.

It was strange that he had not seen it before, for the two women were both pretty and well-endowed with flesh. Miss Piggott was what Mrs Tyzack must have been fifteen or twenty years before. Strapp shrugged. You couldn't really call this faithlessness on the part of the murdered man. In taking a new woman, he had simply renewed his marriage. In a way of speaking, Tyzack had brought his property up to date.

Strapp remained in the periphery of Mabbatt's questioning. He took notes discreetly as the Superintendent gradually lost his temper.

'Why should Mr Tyzack leave you such a large sum?' Mabbatt began.

Jenny Piggott reacted at once:

'You mind your own bloody business!'

'I'm making inquiries into a charge of murder, Miss Piggott!'

'Then go and make them somewhere else if you're going to be nasty! I've had enough, what with the newspaper reporters and all that! *And* telephone calls! I had a dirty old man on just before you

88

came wanting me to move in with him! You want to get hold of that sort of sod before coming around here making out I killed poor Tom!'

The interview was not going well.

It had got off to a bad start, with Mabbatt wishing to establish a connection between the women and Tyzack's acquaintances and friends. Had she ever been to the club?

'No, and I didn't want to! Tom would have taken me. He wasn't ashamed of me. He couldn't, though, not really,' she said illogically. 'But he never took Mrs Tyzack either, so it doesn't mean anything. Of course, she's the one I'm sorry for – she wasn't strong enough to stand up to Tom.'

Mabbatt needled her.

'You were, were you, Miss Piggott?'

The woman dimly recognized his hostility even then.

'Yes! Yes, I suppose so.'

'And which of Mr Tyzack's friends did you entertain here?'

Strapp thought Mabbatt had gone too far.

'Here?'

'Yes,' Mabbatt repeated, making his meaning clearer by spacing his words out carefully. 'Which of Mr Tyzack's friends came here? To see you.'

'To see me?'

She was reluctant to admit to herself the implication of the question.

'You.'

'Why should they come to see me?'

Mabbatt shrugged.

'Tou tell me.'

Jenny Piggott got up from the chintz-covered armchair. There was little fat on her frame. Her arms were not so much plump as solidly cylindrical. She had taken the trouble to put on her make-up, even though she could not have known that Mabbatt and Strapp would visit her that morning. Underneath the brown pancaked coating, her cheeks were dull red.

'I don't know what you mean,' she said.

'I think you do.'

'If I do, I don't like it.'

'This is murder, Miss Piggott.'

'And I had nothing to do with it!'

'You knew the dead man well.'

'And I didn't know his friends – and none of them ever came here! What do you take me for?'

She trembled as she said it. There was no hint of apology in Mabbatt's face. He stuck his great head forward and let his contempt show. Strapp was astonished.

The tension in the large, modern room, with its comfortable furniture of quite a different way of life, had developed to such a fine pitch that at any moment, the hefty Miss Piggott might start a punch-up. You could always tell with women. They shook with nervousness and moral outrage, and their arms went rigid. Before they went into their unco-ordinated attacks, they rolled their eyes and exploded. Mabbatt seemed to want a fight. The woman did too. They stared at one another for a minute.

The woman's face went stiff with anger:

'You're trying to say I had anything to do with Tom's mates? Are you? *Are* you!!'

Her breath was coming in short gasps. Could it be, wondered Strapp, that the two of them got some sort of thrill out of this?'

'*Are* you?' she insisted, facing Mabbatt unsteadily. Mabbatt surrendered.

'I don't see what you mean,' he said. 'Miss Piggott – what can you tell me about Mr Tyzack's friends?'

'Nothing!'

Mabbatt became conciliatory. 'I expect you know Mr Tyzack left you a maggot farm?'

'I don't know and I don't bloody well care! He said he'd always see me right and he told me he'd set me up in business. A *what* farm?'

It was more curiosity than cupidity that moved her.

'Maggot.'

'Maggots? Worms?'

'That's right,' Mabbatt said.

90

'You're having me on!'

Jenny Piggott was annoyed and puzzled.

Strapp had to explain:

'It's a middle-sized business in a bit of land, Miss Piggott. It isn't a secret. You inherit a breeding-farm for maggots – they're bred for bait. Exported all over Europe. It's a handy income.'

Jenny Piggott still thought she was being got at.

'It's a funny thing to leave me.'

'It's quite true,' said Strapp. 'Isn't it, sir?'

'Tom had some funny ideas,' Jenny said, beginning to accept the idea.

Mabbatt then asked why Tom Tyzack should leave her such a large sum. His tone of voice suggested that her inheritance was out of proportion to the services she had rendered during Tyzack's lifetime.

'You mind your own bloody business!' Miss Piggott told him, and the interview was at an end.

Fifteen

'It is permissible to play . . . golf . . . while on a business trip . . .'

At Wolvers the air was clear and the sun had broken through the heavy mist. Root stood on the ninth tee, unaware of Elaine Bliss's indulgent stare. He missed her cheerful wave as she turned to make her husband's breakfast. It had been a busy morning. With the search under way satisfactorily, Bickerdike decided to begin the tiresome job of checking witnesses' statements.

Although Mabbatt had already walked over the section of the course where the murder had been committed, they had been ordered to re-check witnesses' positions at the time of the murder. And so Root had begun by taking Bickerdike from the first tee down to the first green. Root's own neatly-typed statement fluttered on Bickerdike's file.

'You could see down the whole length of the fairway?' asked Bickerdike.

'I watched for at least five minutes before the murder,' Root told him. 'More like ten. Nothing, nobody, crossed into the spinney. I'd have seen.'

'Lecky agrees. He wasn't watching the whole time, though?'

'He had a look at Elaine Bliss.'

'He stayed after all the other members had gone home. He didn't leave till after dark.'

'Oh?'

'I thought Sunday was his first time here.'

'It was.'

'He's worked fast.'

'Aye,' said Root. Lecky had been very quick off the mark. It didn't seem right for the two of them to have begun something on the day of a murder. It was Sunday too.

'Good luck to him,' said Bickerdike, surprisingly.

'Aye.'

They walked on together.

'Who's your money on?' Bickerdike asked.

'For the job?'

'I like the steward.'

'Bliss!' exclaimed Root. 'Charlie Bliss!'

'I'll tell you why. Mabbatt's gone very tender with him so far — hardly what you'd call an interview. He'll have a go at him soon. He likes to keep them stewing, does Mabbatt.'

They reached the green and compared the statements of Cathcart's old fourball with what they themselves could see.

'Right enough,' said Bickerdike. 'They have a clear view of the northern approaches to the spinney. And they didn't see anyone who shouldn't have been there. This one,' he said, pointing to a brief statement, 'confirms Mrs Steel as in view seconds before the murder. He says he was putting and he happened to look up as he was swinging. Her sweater distracted him. He didn't hear the yell, but another of the fourball heard it just as he grumbled about the woman.'

It was a job that had to be done, and the two men tackled it with the same dogged conscientiousness that had gone into the search. Walking to the next vantage point, the second tee, Root said:

'I can't see Bliss knocking Tom on the head.'

'He's got a vicious streak in him, that one. I've seen his kind before. They put up with their wives running around for just so long, then – look out !'

Root revolved the problem around his head. Bliss; Church; Parsons; and Frank. All of them in the spinney. More and more it looked as though Frank Bell had become the choice of the investigating team, whatever Bickerdike said about Bliss. There was the business of the golf-ball against him : that, and the way he had acted in the clubhouse. Mabbatt was to get expert advice that afternoon on Frank's invention. A man from Penfold had promised to come up from the factory to look at the ball which had been found in the dead man's pocket.

'No,' said Root, 'not Bliss. He'd have had to get under the side of the tent, then slide through the undergrowth without being seen by anyone in the spinney. It's possible, but he would have been spotted.'

'We'll check on it after we've had a look from each of the witnesses' positions.'

Just before twelve o'clock they reached the ninth tee. Teams of searching policemen could be seen advancing in line, through the woods to the left of the first tee and to the north of the first green. It was easy enough work, for the winter's fall of leaves was well rotted down; and where grass grew in the woods it was long, straggly growth reaching upwards for the sun. There were a few rabbit-holes and more rat-holes. These were inspected, and the position noted for later scanning by the metal-detector. Bickerdike watched the progress of the teams from time to time. He wanted no relaxation of their vigilance. Mabbatt loathed slackness.

He regarded the map of the spinney and its environs.

'Bliss couldn't have been seen from here,' he said. 'See. There's a patch of gorse concealing the rear of the tent. He could have crawled out and been in the spinney in what ? Three seconds ?'

'Easily.'

'By his own admission, he would have been able to hear Tyzack in there. He said he knew someone had lost a ball by the noise.'

'There's that,' admitted Root.

'So he could have done it.'

'Yes,' said Root.

'Mabbatt'll get it out of him. Right. What can we see from here?'

They could see what the waiting fourball had been able to see. More, in fact, for it was a brighter morning altogether.

'One by one,' said Sergeant Bickerdike, in his rapid Geordie speech. 'You read, I'll check.'

They re-created the Sunday Medal Round. The four on the ninth tee had not watched the spinney all the time. One of them had teed up his ball and tried a few practice-swings at the side of the tee. He had looked from time to time to see what progress Tyzack, Purseglove, Church and Bell were making. He would allow them five minutes in which to find the lost ball – that was the rule. He could see Des Purseglove standing outside the spinney in his reddish anorak. His companions likewise. They had seen a flash of movement in the greenery – one thought he saw a canary yellow jumper, another thought he saw someone in a suit.

'That would be Church and the scrounger. Williamson always wears the same suit – darkish, probably navy-blue originally. No mention of Bliss.'

'And no one saw either Bell or Church.'

'No.'

'Nor Tyzack.'

'No.'

'Nor Parsons.'

Bickerdike screwed his eyes to blot out some of the sunlight. The sun was almost directly overhead.

'They should have seen something.'

'It was dull yesterday morning.'

'Even so!'

'They wouldn't be taking much notice of what went on in the spinney. They'd be waiting for someone to come out. When Tom yelled they'd think he'd got the ball. Then they saw Des Purseglove go into the spinney.'

Bickerdike said:

'I'm bloody starving.'

'So am I.'

'We'll check the remaining fairway, then we'll have a drink and a sandwich.'

Root pointed to a lorry which had crunched its way over the loose gravel drive to the front of the clubhouse.

'The beer's come.'

Bickerdike grinned. His cadaverous face showed signs of animation for the first time that day.

'Now, isn't that good timing, man! I'll buy you one as soon as we're done.'

Root took one last look at the spinney. He had a mental image of the lay-out of that moment in time when the eerie scream had signalled Tyzack's exit from South Yorkshire. Parsons stooping for a plastic practice-ball down at the bottom of the copse. Williamson not more than a few yards away. Both of them screened from the three searching golfers. Bliss, either drinking beer in his tent as he claimed, or moving like a vicious snake through the undergrowth.

Root lengthened his stride to match Bickerdike's. He could see Parsons returning from his morning practice round. The pro was still flexing his wrists for the secret of more power. A wider arc, Parsons had recommended.

'Sergeant!' called Root, his mind made up.

He had considered taking up Mabbatt's suggestion – no, order! – that he play golf whilst at the club.

'Aye, man?'

'I'll play a few holes after lunch, if that's all right with you. Get the feel of the course again.'

Bickerdike was puzzled for a moment. Then he too recalled Mabbatt's instructions.

'I never thought I'd live to see the day,' was all he could say. 'Why, it's a canny job, the police these days!'

Sixteen

'... the player shall not use any artificial devices ... which might assist him ...'

The pathologist's report and the man from the golf-ball manufacturers were waiting for Mabbatt. The pathologist had found seven severe injuries, any one of which could have caused death. His opinion was that a man of normal strength could have inflicted the injuries. He needn't have been particularly powerful, for the weapon used was sharp-edged and probably made of hard steel. There was nothing to suggest that anything but Tom Tyzack's own expensive and missing pitching-wedge had killed him.

'Aye,' Mabbatt said.

He and Strapp were having a beer and a sandwich in the bar-lounge. 'What about this golf-ball firm?'

Bliss was waiting to join the conversation.

'Over there, Sir,' he said, pointing to a young man who was reading a golf magazine.

Mabbatt introduced himself.

'What can you tell me, sir?'

'Oh, we're interested all right! Have to be if anything new turns up. The magic ball that finds itself! We've tried everything from magnetic cores to homing beams. Paints, covers, solid cores. Everything. But the technology moves on and sometimes we dust off the failed experiments to see if anything fits the second time round. I've had a look at the ball you left. Chap who brewed the paint might have something. We'd have got round to trying this kind of paint – it's a neat idea – in time. There's a significant gain in light-reflection that could make all the difference if your ball's lying three-quarters hidden in the rough. Doubt if it's original enough to patent, though it could be.'

'Worth what?' Mabbatt wanted to know.

'Not my line. But money if it came off. And if the Patents Office would accept the idea.'

Mabbatt grinned.

'Have a drink, young man. Bliss!'

'Coming, sir!'

Later, Mabbatt detailed Bickerdike for the duty of harassing Frank Bell.

Bickerdike called at eight, taking with him a youngish bearded constable.

Frank was conscious of the untidiness of the room which served his parents as lounge and dining-room. The business which his father had built up from his savings during twenty-five years of Army service had flourished; it had expanded into what had been the lounge. As well as newspapers, toys, sweets, magazines and tobacco, the Bells sold groceries, minor items of haberdashery such as shoe-laces, needles and cottons; fruit; the vegetables the market gardener down the road had left after supplying his own customers; and a score of items like small oil-lamps and flower-seeds. The stock had engulfed all available room.

'Sorry it's a bit of a mess,' said Frank, wondering why he should apologize.

98

Bickerdike began politely.

'Sorry to trouble you again, sir. I thought you might be able to clear up one or two little matters for us.'

Frank thought of Margaret's fiery encouragement. They had made love the previous evening because they needed each other. 'Don't let them see you're upset again, Frank! Don't let them shout at you and push you around! That horrible Mabbatt man will try to bawl you down, so stand up to him!'

And it wasn't like that at all. Here was the almost comically gaunt Geordie sergeant with a constable who had grown a ginger beard. They wanted to talk, quietly and patiently, just as Frank talked to customers who needed calming as they thought of all those wires and spools and tapes which could go wrong and wreck the monthly figures. Frank recognized the technique. It was called gaining the customer's confidence. Start off with a few, simple incontrovertible facts and build on them. Such as 'Your wage costs must increase every few months, sir. We know what the unions are. Now our machines, on the other hand, are actually decreasing in cost. Maintenance is simpler, software cheaper.'

'Let's start with Mr Tyzack, sir,' suggested Bickerdike.

'Yes?'

'It appears that Mr Tyzack had extensive business interests.'

'I've heard that.'

'Your golf-ball, sir. Did you take out patent rights on the invention?'

'No. I thought of it, but I just didn't get around to it.'

'You considered it a valuable property, sir?'

'Not really.'

'Buut you thought it might be valuable eventually?'

Mabbatt had told Bickerdike to go easy. Repeated lines of questioning: always the same – get the lad to think about murder. Get him to worry about being caught out.

'I'd no way of knowing.'

'You've a good deal of business experience yourself, Mr Bell. Surely you must have some idea of the value of your invention?'

'Why don't you ask the experts?'

Bickerdike nodded his head.

'Superintendent Mabbatt did that today, sir.'

'And?'

'I'm not at liberty to divulge the information, sir. I'd like to know if Mr Tyzack thought your invention to be of value.'

'Tom couldn't know! How could he?- I didn't know if it would work properly in all light conditions. How could he? I'd only just got them from the glass technology people.'

'At Kenyon's, sir.'

Frank remembered Mabbatt's grim insistence during the awful interview on the afternoon of the murder. Again and again, the grating voice had hammered away at the single point: why should the ball be in Tyzack's pocket!

'Yes. I've a friend there. He and I think that the kind of paint we dreamt up gives nearly twenty-five per cent more reflection in normal lighting conditions. And that's just a start.'

'Did Mr Tyzack know the figure you mentioned?'

'Yes.'

'When did you discuss it with him?'

'I didn't discuss it – it came out in casual conversation. Maybe when we were changing, maybe in the bar.'

'And when was the last time you talked about the ball, sir?'

'I told you – yesterday morning!'

'And that was the last time you discussed the subject?'

'Yes.'

'No more was said of it?'

'No!'

'And you didn't see anything of Mr Tyzack once you were in the spinney?'

And so it went on. The pattern did not change. From fact to opinion, from known pin-pointed movements to conjecture, from words recorded to possible interpretations of them. After an hour of it, Frank's mother looked in. Margaret had arrived.

Bickerdike excused himself, refused the tea which Mrs Bell had made, and went on his way. When he and the silent plainclothesman had gone, Frank's parents stared at him with a pity that almost reduced him to tears. Margaret tried to hide her own melting feelings; she was unsuccessful. They all drank tea in an atmosphere of fear-laden sympathy.

Bickerdike was ordered to keep up the pressure on the Bell household. There would be several heavy-footed police patrols around that night. Frank could expect to be required to assist the police in their inquiries again very soon.

Seventeen

'The professional holds an advantage over the amateur by reason of having devoted himself to the game . . .'

It was whilst he was waiting to be called at the inquest that Root first admitted to himself his dissatisfaction with Mabbatt's methods of investigation. Two days had passed since Tom Tyzack's killing. During that time, the Superintendent had concentrated on the dead man's background.

He had explored Tyzack's property deals with monumental patience. They revealed the nature of the murdered man. Tom had been a man of instant decision and almost uncannily astute judgement. A piece of land would lie unnoticed by the local entrepreneurs, perhaps because it was covered by the ruins of an old church, or a cinema that bingo could not restore to life. He would chance on it as he roared through the pit-towns in his blue Rover, stop, ring the gilded Robinson in Sheffield and instruct him to offer six hundred or two thousand three hundred and twenty-five — always the *right* amount, never too much. And, in the course of time, the site would blossom as a supermarket or a service station.

Root could admire Mabbatt's thoroughness, but was it right to spend so much time on Tyzack's background?

Surely the people that mattered most were those who had been in the spinney? The people who might have seen something, heard someone. True, Williamson had been examined by a consultant surgeon. His condition was confirmed; it was practically impossible for him to have dealt those savage blows. So Williamson was out of it. Routine, thought Root. Ensuring that the right things were done was a part of ordinary police investigation, however.

The routine things almost looked after themselves – the meticulous cross-checking of statements. Then the equally painstaking investigation of the financial arrangements of Church, Bell, Parsons and Bliss, to establish, if that could be done, a motive of gain through Tom's death. And, naturally, Mabbatt had arranged that they all be chivvied. Each was subjected to a certain amount of discreet harassment. Each received calls to go over this or that point.

Mabbatt had seemed to be in control of the complex operation, and yet Root felt a niggling doubt. Was it because he seemed too confident? Mabbatt was doing all the right things, but was he asking the right people about the murder? He had been ham-fisted with Williamson; he hadn't spent time with the ground-staff; he hadn't wanted to talk to the other scroungers who had been on the course that Sunday. And these were the people who *knew* Wolvers. It was their livelihood.

Root's thoughts were interrupted when he was called. He patted his uniform pocket to make sure that his notebook hadn't fallen out on the way to the nineteenth-century Aldermanic Hall. It was there.

He gave his evidence, was dismissed and listened to the rest of the inquiry into the death of Thomas Geoffrey Tyzack. The coroner was in little doubt.

It was a foul and deadly assault. Never, in his experience, had anyone been murdered while playing golf. He said that there had been violent deaths on the golf course before, of course, and he made reference to the *Golfer's Handbook*. No doubt the violent end of the

103

late Thomas Geoffrey Tyzack would add a melancholy entry to that publication. In the absence of any direct evidence to the contrary, he directed that the jury return a verdict of Murder, by a Person or Persons Unknown. And God Save the Queen.

They all went back to Wolvers after the inquest.

Mabbatt was in a surprisingly good humour. He talked amiably to Root about Tyzack's business ventures, and it was clear that he had some admiration for his methods. Then he looked down the glorious first fairway:

'Enjoying you holiday, Root?'

'Sir?'

'You like being here, don't you?'

'Yes, sir.'

'You've had a game of golf, haven't you?'

'Yes, sir.'

Strapp had accompanied him around the course on Tuesday afternoon, admiring the efficient way he had punched low shots into the wind. It had been hardly more than extended practice, but Root had to admit to himself that it was golf.

And that was enough.

'Talked much to the members, Root?'

'There haven't been all that many of them in, sir.'

'Keep at it! Someone knows something they haven't let on about yet. Secretive bastards! Listen to 'em, Root – listen to 'em when they think there's no one listening. When they've had a few beers.'

'That'll be on Saturday, sir. At the Irish match.'

But Mabbatt didn't want to know about the annual fixture.

'What's this Irish Match?' Strapp asked later.

Root explained:

'That's what we call the game we play on Saturday. It isn't real golf. For a start, we play across the entire course as though it was a single hole. And there's fifty of us.'

He showed Strapp what he meant. The greatest distance that could be achieved on the course lay between two points; the seventeenth tee and the fourth green.

'To make it harder?' asked Strapp, who was beginning to appreciate what was meant by an Irish match.

'Longer. Harder. And dafter. You have to cross about a mile of broken country — roads, ditches, two streams, thickets, and the clubhouse, that is, if you take the direct line.'

He pointed to the map again.

'We begin here, all fifty of us. Each man takes his own line — some stick to the seventeenth fairway and then try to carry the road and the thick gorse to the right of the tenth fairway and then across to the ninth. That way means blasting over the wood. It needs quite a bit of judgement.'

'And they have a few jars first?'

'That's part of the idea. It isn't anything like any golf match you've ever seen!'

Root became enthusiastic about the affair.

'Fifty men blasting off in all directions! It's the golfing equivalent of the Charge of the Light Brigade. It's the Captain's job to see that everyone has a skinful before we start. You'll have to see it, you will.'

'You say they've closed the club entrance lists?' Strapp put in. He liked what he heard.

'You could apply to go on the waiting list.'

'I might. Let's get back to this Irish match.'

'The only rule is that you're allowed one club — any one you like. Driver. Wedge. Putter. Anything. And you have to hole out. Everyone who enters has to hole out or else contribute a pound to help the Captain pay for the beer.'

'It's an expensive job being Captain.'

'It is.'

'It sounds mad.'

'It is.'

'Tyzack played in it last year, I suppose?'

'Oh, yes. Tom was a sport.'

Root could visualize Tom Tyzack, full of beer and raucous, vulgar humour, pushing his way through the crowd to be amongst the leaders.

'Did he win?'

'Well, no,' said Root.

'Who won?'

'Well, as a matter of fact, I did.'

'Bugger me,' said Strapp in admiration. 'How many strokes?'

'It wasn't a course record. I took a six-iron.'

'How many?'

'Seventeen.'

'It sounds a lot. It isn't all that far.'

'Parsons took thirty-one. He lost two balls trying to hit over the wood I told you about.'

'What about Tyzack?'

'He didn't finish. He had to have a sleep at the beer tent. Elaine Bliss had a few crates of beer ready for us, and that was as far as he got.'

'So the match goes on this year?'

'Oh yes. Mr Church called in whilst you were out. Everything's on. The Captain's Match, the Dance – Saturday.'

Strapp paused.

'Where do I apply for membership?'

'See Mr Church. Or I will, if you like,' said Root. He would put in a word for Strapp. That would help.

Root wondered whether to voice his doubts about the investigation. His training won, and he kept silent. After all, he told himself, if he couldn't get on to a thief who was stealing house-bricks despite regular surveillance of the site, what could he offer in a case of murder? It wasn't as though he had anything but a vague consciousness of unease; how could he go to Mabbatt and say, 'Excuse me, sir, I think you're taking too much for granted! Or, 'Don't you think you should think about the suspects as people, sir, rather than as bank balances? And: 'What about the humbler folk, sir: why not talk to them again?' He'd be wrong, of course, because it stood out like a sore thumb that Mabbatt had to cover the more or less normal eventualities like who stood to gain, or who could have been sufficiently angered by Tom to commit murder. To himself he muttered:

'It's just that I can't see Frank hurting anybody – nor Parsons.

Nor Church. Nor even Charlie Bliss!'

He stopped himself.

He didn't know the minds of any one of those who had been in the spinney sufficiently well to judge. Not a single one of them. And as for how the wedge came to disappear he could not begin to hazard a guess. He determined, however, that if the chance offered itself, he would do what his instincts prompted: talk to Williamson again.

On Thursday, Parsons demanded the wedge he had loaned. Root was outside the professional's shop at the time. Mabbatt was on his way to interview Bliss when Parsons stopped him:

'Got your man yet?' he called from his shop.

Mabbatt glowered.

'No.'

'He's making you sweat, then.'

'Excuse me, sir.'

'Just a minute. You've got a club of mine. I'd like it back – makes the shop look untidy, having a set on display one club short. You must have finished with it by now?'

'Get it, Sergeant,' Mabbatt told Strapp.

But Parsons kept him.

'The Penfold man came to see me about the golf-ball on Monday. That idea of Frank Bell's – it could be a winner.'

Mabbatt stopped and turned to face Parsons. The muscular little pro grinned. He enjoyed confrontations with bigger men. Cocky, completely sure of his place in his own circle, he deferred to no one. Root knew that this was the reason for his success with a certain kind of woman in the golfing world. Mabbatt would be thinking about the deserted family that Parsons never spoke of; and of the wealthy Mrs Steel and her hard, bright abrasive laughter.

'It's interesting to hear your opinion, sir. Did you ever speak to Mr Tyzack about the invention?'

Parsons laughed aloud.

'You're barking up the wrong tree again! Jack Parsons is all right for a bob or two – I don't need to pinch Frank's idea!'

'Well, sir, did you?'

Parsons shook his head.

'Frank talked to me about it, but I didn't think there was anything in it. I listened to him, just as I'd listen to anyone's ideas. They come in with all sorts of suggestions. Why, even Dr Fordham thinks he's got an invention that's going to sweep the golf markets.'

'What's that, then, sir?'

'Nothing to do with findable golf-balls! You'll have to ask him yourself — he mightn't like it if I told you.'

Root waited as the two men faced one another. He shifted the collar of his old-fashioned raincoat so that it kept out the thin driving rain. Out of the course only two or three couples, and one solitary individual, were playing. The fairways were heavy with rain; the big elms rang with the noise of wet rooks. Root looked up as an upstairs window slammed shut. Elaine Bliss was keeping out the cold, damp air.

At last Mabbatt said:

'You'll let me know if you think of anything else, sir?'

'I'll do that. I'll do that at once.'

'Let's see what Bliss has to say,' Mabbatt said to Strapp. 'Root — talk to him.' He indicated the broad back of the professional. 'He's said nothing so far.'

'Yes, sir.' Root felt sorry for Charlie Bliss.

'And go into the bar.'

'Sir.'

Root was keeping a careful note of his expenses. So far, he had spent more than four pounds on drinks, much too much for a family man. Then there was petrol for the ancient Hillman, since the bus service was not satisfactory. Root had waited for hours the previous evening, only to discover that the local bus crews were staging a go-slow strike in support of their colleagues in Bradford. Finally, a police-car had passed, and he had stopped it with a despairing and ridiculous waving of hands. His wife had told him to use the car after that. Four pounds spent on drinks he hadn't particularly wanted, for there was a dismal atmosphere in the bar. Charlie Bliss was moping. His face hurt, and his wife talked too much. None of the members particularly wished conversation with the steward; none bought him drinks. Root, a sociable man but no extrovert, drank with this or that member who happened to need a reviver after a round of golf, but always in a funereal manner; Tom Tyzack's spirit lingered in the huge room. So Root drank economically during the five or six hours to ten o'clock; mostly beer, mostly unwanted. Four pounds on beer, he noted, one pound and seventy-five pence on petrol. Could he make a claim for his ticket and drinks at the Captain's Dance? Not for his wife, of course; but he himself had been ordered to attend, and that surely was duty?

The result of his socializing had been nil. Root told himself that he was glad he hadn't put himself forward for detective work.

He went to talk to the professional. Parsons grumbled interminably about the state of the course and the shortage of caddies.

'All that turned up was one daft lad, and your lot chased *him* off!'

Root left him to his sour grievances.

Eighteen

'If the opponent give wrong information . . . and correct his mistake
. . . he shall incur no penalty ; . . .'

'Ah, Superintendent !' Bliss said, trying to inject a note of welcome
and hospitality through his pained mouth. 'Can I get you a drink ?'

'No, Mr Bliss.'

'Tea ? Elaine's upstairs. I can ask her to make some.'

'Come up to the Secretary's office.'

Bliss smiled confidentially :

'I'd be very glad to give you any help I can, sir ! It's a nasty
business, what with poor Mr Tyzack dead and everyone talking.'

He let the last word hang in the air as they progressed up the stately stairway, past the dim oils and along the wide, high corridor, built
to take the traffic of scores of servants in the opulent days of the Hall.

'Like, I mean,' said Bliss, still trying for the role of intimate, 'if
there's anything else you want to know ?'

'Sit down.'

110

'Only there hasn't been much business this week, and I could count on the fingers of one hand the customers we've had in each night for drinks. Did you find what you were searching for, sir? Out on the course? The golf-club? Parsons told me about it. I didn't mean to pry. You know he's leaving at the end of the month?'

Mabbatt ignored him.

Strapp, who had seated himself by the door, knew how Mabbatt would proceed. This was no Jenny Piggott or Parsons. The steward, with his ingratiating, bruised face and ready, toothy smile, would be given every chance to relieve his conscience. Mabbatt wanted him eliminated, if that was possible. Cleared. Or a confession.

'You were there!' suddenly growled Mabbatt.

He thumped a fist down on to the map of the spinney.

Bliss looked at the tiny neat blue tent.

'Yes!'

He was agitated already. His chin quivered, and his neat hands trembled.

'You said you heard voices.'

'I did!'

'Whose?'

'I don't know – you know they call to one another. Things like "Did you get a line?" and "Found it yet?"'

'Who said that? Thomas Tyzack?'

'No one said it – I'm just guessing.'

'You're concealing evidence, Bliss!'

And there it was. Naked, accusing, loud-voiced, the rage of authority. Bliss shook.

'I never! I never did! I told you all I knew! I told you about the Committee – all of them! I tried to help. That's all I wanted to do! Help!'

It sounded like a plea. Strapp, scribbling smoothly, had just a little sympathy for the fat little man. Mabbatt's pig's eyes were fixed on the quivering man's face. Strapp wondered if Mabbatt could be right after all: surely no one could look so guilty and still be innocent?

'You said you were in the tent!'

'I was!'

'You were seen out of it!'

'Well, I went out to have a look!'

'You didn't tell me your wife was Tyzack's fancy woman!'

'I –'

'Did you!'

'No!'

'Why not? She was, wasn't she?'

'I didn't know about it!'

'You did!'

'It doesn't matter anyway!'

'It does to me!'

'She only told me after he was dead!'

'You're lying!'

'I'm not!'

'You are, you little bloody ponce!'

'You've no right to call me names!'

'You – little – bloody – ponce!' bawled Mabbatt, spacing out the words. 'Ponce! Poncing for your wife!'

Bliss looked around wildly at Strapp.

'I did all I could to help! I told you about that lad – he did it! He killed Tom! And he hit me – he only hit me because I told you about him! And Parsons said I needed hitting, and he threatened me, and there's a law against it!'

Strapp wrote that the steward had expressed a desire to co-operate.

'You knew she was having it off with him! Before the murder – you were in the tent! You knew he was in the spinney! You knew you could get there without being seen! You saw your wife out there laughing at you!'

'She wasn't laughing at me! She's a liar! I didn't know about Tom Tyzack, nor Mr Church! She told me afterwards!'

'Liar!'

Mabbatt smashed his hand down on the desk, which solidly absorbed the punch. A pen shot up into the air and landed on Bliss's lap. Its touch drove him almost to hysteria.

'Well, I had to!' he screamed. 'I had to! She said they'd have me

112

out of here.' Where would I get a job at my age? I had to! And anyway, there's no harm!'

He pleaded with Mabbatt.

'I mean, I'm not as young as I was. And they were all gentlemen — except *him*!'

Mabbatt grinned evilly.

'And he'd have put you on the street if you'd opened your mouth!'

It fitted, thought Strapp. Bliss was an idler; he was in the easiest job he could find. He had a position of authority and he had made the best of it. No doubt he fed and drank well; and certainly he had luxurious surroundings. If all that were threatened, it made for a powerful motive.

Bliss had gone white.

'Yes!' he whispered. 'Elaine said so!'

'Your own wife, eh?'

Bliss stared at Mabbatt. Poor sod, thought Root, as he jotted down questions and answers.

'So you were in the spinney?' said Mabbatt conversationally.

Bliss's normal colour had gone. He was a grey-white figure. His bare arms and his nervous, woman's hands, as well as his face, had turned ashen. Strapp saw that Mabbatt's question had not penetrated his misery.

'I had to shut my eyes,' the steward said.

'You got out through the back?'

'But she didn't mean it — I mean, she said he'd have taken her away with him, but how could he when he was dead?'

Mabbatt tried again:

'You saw him bending over?'

Bliss blinked. He turned again to Strapp, and, talking as if to one who might have control over an elemental force, he said:

'Tell him I didn't! I only put my head out of the tent! I were frightened of Mr Tyzack! I couldn't have — *couldn't*! He were so big!'

Mabbatt sighed. He gave up, and Strapp could see that he was not entirely disappointed.

'See if you can get us some tea, will you please, Mr Bliss? You've

113

been very helpful. As usual.'

Strapp was not surprised at the blush of pleasure on the face of the steward.

'Any time, sir! Any time.'

Elaine Bliss put the phone down as Bliss came into the apartment at a trot. She faced him equably with a smile. If he had seen the adoring look that had transfigured her as she talked to Jack Lecky, he would have known at once that he had lost her.

'Make a pot of tea, love,' he told her. 'Be quick, it's for the police.'

She whirled his fat little frame around. For a moment he thought she was attacking him.

'All right, Charlie! Who's a nice little chubby lad, then!'

Bliss responded to the familiar endearment:

'Me! Charlie Bliss!'

A man of shallow emotions, he felt as happy as five minutes before he had been in despair. With Tyzack out of the way and Church under his wife's thumb, all that business of keeping out of the apartment might be over.

'I think I'll get a new dress for Saturday!' Elaine called. 'I've got the money from Christmas.' She meant the members' contributions to the Gratuities Fund. 'Shall I get black again, Charlie?'

'No! Have a change, love. Get something bright – it's time we all stopped being gloomy, 'Laine!'

In the Secretary's office Mabbatt gave instructions for Church to be questioned again.

'Be bloody careful,' he told Bickerdike. 'He's a man with connections.'

'Yes, sir,' Bickerdike said stolidly. 'I'll go steady.'

'Not too steady,' Mabbatt said. 'Careful.'

'Nothing more on Bell, sir?' asked Bickerdike.

'Nowt.'

Mabbatt relapsed into glumness. He heaped sugar into Elaine Bliss's best china cups. Root and Sergeant Bickerdike went out of the room.

'Still fancy the steward?' Root asked Bickerdike.

114

Both had heard a brief account of Bliss's questioning.

'We'll crack it,' Bickerdike said. 'We'd better, man. Mabbatt's to see the Chief Constable Saturday morning. You'd best be on the golf course for that bloody silly game Strapp told me about. Early. You might be wanted.'

Nineteen

'The Committee shall make and publish Local Rules for abnormal conditions . . .'

It was the day of the Irish match. And the Dance. The warm weather had returned. Over the green course, rolling white clouds spun about a brilliant blue sky. The elms swayed in the light winds. Wolvers Hall showed up foursquare and noble in the July sunlight. The fairways had resumed their luxurious greenness as a result of the week's rains. The greens − newly-cut − were tiny sand-edged emeralds. The ground staff had been hard at work tidying an immaculate course. There was an air of pleased expectancy at Wolvers, and, to Root, it was obvious that the pall of gloom that had hung over the club since Tom Tyzack's death was now dispersed. Tom was buried at Wickinglow. Wreaths had been sent, the widow officially consoled. Both the Secretary and the Captain had attended the funeral. Now that he was underground, Tom could be talked about. Tom saying this, doing that; the reputable things, of course. Tom's scandals would be the subject of discussion later when the Captain's Dance was in full swing.

As instructed, Root had arrived at the course rather early for the Irish match. He met Fordham in the locker-room.

'Hello, Arthur! You playing in the match? I've just knocked round the back six on my own. Ah! Knew there was something! You found a club-head in the spinney, didn't you? You did, you know, Arthur!'

Root wondered how he knew.

'It wasn't what we were looking for.'

'I can tell you whose it was!'

Root's professional interest was aroused.

'Superintendent Mabbatt would be interested.'

'I doubt it, lad. It's been there since the year after the General Strike.'

Root did his sums.

'Nineteen twenty-seven?'

'It was a man called Lightfoot, Captain Lightfoot. He'd fought at Gallipoli. He was a sandy little man. A very fine golfer indeed. We were on the twelfth green, and it was his putt. It was raining at the time. He's been dead twenty or more years. He was just going to take his putt when a rabbit ran across the green. A big one. They used to be common here. It came out of the wood near the Hall, then straight across the green. Knocked Lightfoot's ball away, banged into my partner's bag. We didn't have trolleys then. Off it shot into the spinney at the back of the twelfth. Captain Lightfoot – Jeremy, I think we called him – chased off after it. When he couldn't see it, he threw his putter after it. We never did find it.'

'I'll tell the Superintendent,' said Root.

Fordham smiled.

'Finding CID work a bit much, Arthur?'

'You get used to your own patch.'

'You'll be back soon.'

'I hope so!'

More members arrived. Root and Fordham went out to the beer tent. Jack Lecky was there. Fordham recognized him:

'Hello! Playing in the match?'

'He's not eligible,' Root said. 'Jack's application is up on the board.'

'I'm walking round with Arthur,' Lecky told Fordham.

'Well, it's a good day for it.'

He would have said the same if it had rained frogs.

Just then, Elaine Bliss arrived.

She smiled at Lecky.

An ordinary Yorkshire girl, he thought. Why hadn't he married one like this instead of a nervous schoolmistress? She contrived to brush against him and he thought of the tower-room and its faded paintings.

'I hope you're staying for the Dance,' she said.

'I wouldn't miss it.'

'I'll see you later.'

'Yes.'

Lecky was amazed at his good fortune. This woman was all he wanted from life. And golf.

Groups of golfers began to form. Each was certain of the merits of the club he carried. Most chose a medium-iron.

Root half-listened. He went over the arrangements his wife had made. The older boy was sufficiently responsible to look after his brother and sisters; Ursula would be at the little village hairdresser's, where she would have her beautiful red hair twisted into the latest style as interpreted by Miss Cross. He thought of her with great affection. He had met her the first time he had gone out on patrol in South Yorkshire, and both of them had known at once that they would be married. The joke they could both laugh at was at the way of their meeting. He had had to ask the way to one of the local schools, and she was the person he stopped. She had been at the grammar-school still, a leggy prefect in the sixth form. Marriage had prevented her from going to university. She hadn't regretted it. Root was sure of it. He thought of his wife with great pride. Ursula – for years she had apologized for her un-Yorkshire name – would arrive at about eight-thirty. Till then, there was time for a beer or two, the Irish match, a shower, and then a chat with Mabbatt. He corrected himself. No one chatted with Mabbatt: a report to the Superintendent.

It had been arranged that Mabbatt be invited, though on the understanding that he keep in the background.

'I'm buggered if I want to see how they carry on,' he had told Root, 'but you never know. It'll be the first time they've had a chance to talk to one another since the crime. I want to watch faces. You do the same. And listen!'

Root put Mabbatt out of his mind. Joe Fordham was quite right about his wanting to get back to the village. There were things that the new man wouldn't know about, couldn't be expected to know about. Police-constable Hunt was a youngish, rather ambitious officer; he'd want to find the prowler who was raiding the garages for tools. He'd know how to set about it too. And the brick-thief. But he wouldn't know how to handle Syd Smethurst's lad, who was getting pills from somewhere. Root tried to recall what had been the equivalent in his own teenage days: playing chicken on motor-bikes? Swilling five or six pints of beer on a Saturday night? Nowadays, the kids discounted courage as well as capacity. Root hoped that Hunt wouldn't lean too hard on the boy. It would only make him run, and then it would be a matter for social workers, probation officers and a juvenile court. How *did* the brick-thief get them away?

He saw Elaine Bliss brush quite deliberately against Jack Lecky; there was almost a flash of electricity between them. Root looked away. He didn't approve, though he could understand. He had seen too much of the results of marital unhappiness to criticize Lecky's decisions. Or Elaine's.

The groups of golfers began to converge on the beer tent. It was time for the Captain to buy.

Harry Tufnell ran a successful used-car business. Unlike most car salesmen known to Root, Tufnell was a modest, retiring man. His golf was almost unbelievably bad. Every time he made a particularly bad stroke, he would say, 'I don't know how I did it!' And his partners would agree.

'Right, lads!' Tufnell called. 'Drink what you can in a quarter of

119

an hour, then off to the seventeenth tee! One club, you count your own strokes, go any way you like – no lifting anywhere, no out of bounds, no bloody cheating! Start serving, Charlie!' he added to Bliss.

To yells of approval the business of getting through the crates of beer got under way; Root felt himself becoming infected by the competitiveness of it all. There were, perhaps, three hundred bottles of beer. If you didn't get your share there was something wrong with you.

'Don't hang back, lad,' Tufnell called happily to Jack Lecky.

'I'm not a member yet.'

'Not to worry – come *on*, lad!'

Twenty

'The player is not of necessity entitled to see the ball when playing a stroke.'

Half-an-hour later the Irish match began. Many of the members not in the match had come to see the start.

Lecky saw a number of people he knew. The Secretary was clutching an eight-iron. Church had drunk a good deal, but he was still worried about some point of organization. Near him was another member of the Sunday fourball, Des Purseglove. Elaine Bliss had come to watch. She waved to him. Lecky made up his mind in that moment.

With a bit of luck, the divorce would be finalized in a few months. Elaine was the most comfortable woman he had ever met. He waved back.

'Thy's chancing thi arm!' a complete stranger said to him. 'Thy aren't on t'Committee!'

It was the beer talking. Lecky didn't care. He knew exactly what the stranger meant, and he simply didn't care.

'What if I am?' he asked. 'You would if you had half a chance.'

The stranger was delighted. A grizzled, thickset man in checked plus-fours, he laughed his pleasure aloud. Then he slapped Lecky on the back.

'You do right, lad! You do!'

These Yorkshiremen, thought Lecky: uncouth, bloody-minded and presumptuous. They ran clean contrary to the general run of Englishmen.

Harry Tufnell yelled incomprehensibly from the seventeenth tee. Church tried to usher the milling crowd into a line.

'Wheer's thi club, lad?' the stranger wanted to know.

'He isn't playing,' Root told him. 'It's Fred Aspinall,' he added, turning to Lecky. 'Pay no attention. He's got the stuff running out of his ears.'

The grizzled man offered Lecky a drink from a half-bottle of whisky.

'I will,' said Lecky. 'Gladly!'

Uncouth, presumptuous and generous. He made up his mind to drink a good deal before he went to meet Elaine in the painted tower. He drank from the warm bottle.

Aspinall watched.

'Tha does right!' he bawled. 'But steady does it – don't empty t'bottle!'

'Ready!' yelled Tufnell. 'Don't kill any bugger – watch where you're hitting!'

'We'll keep well back,' Root told Lecky. 'We always have to patch somebody up.'

'Right! We're off!' called Tufnell. 'After me, lads!'

It was his right to drive off first.

He swung hugely at the ball, disturbed it slightly, and fell flat on his face.

'He's not hit it!' Church called, as the others, trying to hold themselves upright through their laughter, teed up their balls. 'We can't start yet – he isn't off! It's against the rules!'

'Rules be buggered!' bawled Aspinall. 'Stand away!'

122

He was using a wood. Whilst the rest of the mob scrambled for an advantageous position somewhere in line with the seventeenth tee, and as Tufnell got to his feet in an alcoholic haze, Aspinall swung crisply and smacked his ball across to the fifteenth fairway. It was the signal for two score or so of golf-balls to be sliced, hooked, squeezed, muffed, thinned and topped in the general direction of the clubhouse and, beyond that and hidden from view by numerous obstacles, the fourth green. Lecky saw Aspinall run off through a storm of descending golf-balls.

He took another large pull at the whisky. It was two-thirds full.

'I've still got the bottle!' he said aloud to Root.

Root grinned.

'Pass it over.'

They had a large drink, and then Root waited for a gap in the scurrying, swaying mob that was already scattering widely over the various fairways. He teed the new ball up. Then he swung back, a short, powerful, relaxed backswing. Lecky saw that it was perfect: Root's right elbow pointed to the ground. He swung through. Root hit a sweet shot a hundred and fifty yards towards the seventeenth green.

A surprisingly strong gust of wind held the ball so that it dropped steeply. It pitched and bounced twice.

'Very nice,' said Lecky.

'Good shot!' called Elaine Bliss.

'Where's my bloody ball?' Tufnell asked.

She helped him to set up the tee again.

'Three off the tee,' he said. 'I don't know how I did it! Can't have been concentrating.'

Root and Lecky automatically moved behind Tufnell; with some players, you couldn't be sure that the ball would go forward. But Tufnell connected, sending a three-iron shot screwing wildly about a hundred yards towards the fifteenth green.

'I'm going that way, Arthur!' he said to Root. 'That's the best line – down the fifteenth, across to the tenth, carry the eleventh, and over the woods!'

'We'll see you later, Harry!'

He grinned at Lecky. As Tufnell reeled after his ball, he said:

'At least it can't cost him any more going that way. I've never known him finish the match yet.'

Elaine Bliss came over to see them.

'I'll walk back with you,' she said. 'Well, Arthur, is your Ursula ready for tonight?'

'I hope so.'

'I've got a new dress! Flowered – it's long. It's the first really long dress I've ever had.'

Root knew that she was not talking to him.

Was it such a bad thing for Jack Lecky to take up with her? Who could get hurt? He was on the way to being divorced: she'd been around. If only the black shadow of Tyzack's death wasn't present, it might be a good thing all round. Elaine wasn't used to men like Jack Lecky. Opportunists and creeps, like Tyzack and Charlie Bliss, yes. Pompous asses like Church. But Lecky was different. He had the look of a man who would know how to treat a woman. Root reached his ball, and all thought of marital entanglements went. A hit for distance now. When Fred Aspinall stopped slashing at the turn just in front of him he would hit for the narrow neck of fairway in front of the seventeenth green.

Then it was a matter of finding a way through the swaying, yelling golfers in front of him – neat, low punched shots delicately placed so that they made distance without endangering life and limb. A sudden irate yell in front told him that already someone had been hit by a ball.

'Don't worry!' he told Lecky. 'Dr Fordham's out on the course.'

He himself did worry.

He remembered the death-scream from the spinney. There could be a murderer in that happy, half-drunk mob in front of him.

'A drink?' asked Lecky.

'No, Jack. I've had enough for now.'

'We'll be seeing you later?' Elaine Bliss called to them as she made for the clubhouse.

'You will,' promised Lecky.

'All right!' called Root.

124

She exaggerated the swaying of her well-shaped hips as she went; Root watched her for a minute or so. Had someone killed Tyzack because of that sensuous figure? He tried to shake off the tendrils of dizziness that kept forming and writhing through his brain; he had drunk far too much. This wasn't the way to accumulate information. He looked at the widespread field. Aspinall was out of sight. Church was arguing with a bunch of friends who had decided to stick together no matter what. Already one man was making for the clubhouse, deciding that the heat of the day was too much for him.

'Where to now, Arthur?' asked Jack Lecky.

'Over the back of the seventeenth and out in front of the thirteenth green. I've got to carry the copse, but it isn't a hard shot.'

Lecky laughed.

'I wouldn't fancy it. Not now,' he said, indicating the bottle. Root barely heard him. He was all golfer now, estimating the power of the wind, the height of the tall sycamores in the copse, and the lie of his ball. Fortunately, it had landed on a rough-cut piece of fairway where coarse grass grew thickly. It stood on a little mound of greenery. It would help in gaining additional lift. He addressed himself to the ball.

Dimly he heard Jack Lecky call:

'Bad luck! That'll cost you shots!'

Root looked up at the yell. He could see nothing out of the ordinary. Disasters like shanking and heavy slicing were part of golf's rich pattern. He looked down. The next shot required absolute concentration.

Root swung. For once, his wrists failed him. He sliced heavily into the middle of the copse.

'Damn!' he bawled. 'Just like a beginner!'

'Bugger it!' echoed Tufnell's voice. 'I've done it again!'

Bays and yells took up the shout as fifty inebriated golfers searched or called for an open field, or roared astonishment at their luck. Jack Lecky shook his head. He was drunk. When Purseglove in his reddish jacket had disappeared into the undergrowth alongside the seventeenth fairway, it had disturbed him momentarily. Purseglove had to be out of the running with a shot like that. It was rank bad luck.

Then Aspinall began to yell for his whisky and he forgot about it. 'Wheer's mi bottle?'

'I'll look for my ball,' said Root. 'You'd better take him his booze. He'll stand there all day yelling until he gets it.'

Root blundered about the copse, cursing. It wasn't a hard shot, yet he had muffed it. Stiff wrists, he told himself. Not rolling the wrists and so leaving the club-face open at the point of impact. He deserved to lose it! He slashed at nettles and brambles.

Lecky found the ball as soon as he returned to the copse. It was half-hidden by a fallen rotting branch. A squirrel began to chatter behind them as they examined the lie together.

'I can't hit it on. I'll have to knock it out sideways,' Root groaned.

'That's all you can do, Arthur.'

Root didn't swear often, but he did now. He looked up at the squirrel and cursed it. It watched him until he had finished. Then it flew from its high perch into the largest tree in the copse. Root grinned at Lecky.

'It is a silly bloody game, isn't it?'

They followed the field for ten minutes, and then Root pushed his ball into a bunker guarding the twelfth green. They were near the tent. More than a dozen golfers were glad to stop for another drink.

Parsons was in the beer tent, drinking deeply. Charlie Bliss was holding court, assessing the chances of those who had got to the half-way stage by a more or less direct route. The Secretary refused a drink from three happy golfers. He was still disturbed about the ragged start.

'We can't have that sort of thing at Wolvers!' he exclaimed. 'This isn't some municipal course with gangs of miners roaming over it — we're a private club!'

Aspinall arrived.

'Get me some more bloody balls!' he yelled to Parsons. 'I've lost two buggers already! 'Ave a drink? Some bugger stole me bottle but I got the bugger back!'

Parsons sent his assistant for golf-balls.

Charlie Bliss was quite merry by this time.

126

'Poor old Tom would have liked the turn-out!' he was saying to a bunch of his cronies. 'Never made it last year – got stuck here and passed out. What a man he was!'

Parsons snorted.

'He didn't think much of you, Bliss, you rat-faced bastard! He'd have outed you if it weren't for your missus!'

Bliss pretended he hadn't heard.

'Mr Parsons!' said Church. 'Have some respect!'

Parsons weighed up the red-faced portly figure. Root could see the anger in the professional's eyes: he knew who had been the leading spirit in his dismissal. Church's pretty niece had been for lessons until Parsons had been indiscreet. But the anger died. Parsons was not one to carry a grudge too far. Root repeated the thought and wondered if he was right.

'How many?' Parsons asked him.

'Nine. And I'm in a bunker.'

'Have a beer!'

'I will. How many?'

'Five. I'm lying badly in front of the wood down there.' He indicated the big woods below the spinney in which Tom Tyzack had been killed.

Golfers arrived, drank more beer, and proceeded with much self-congratulation towards the fourth green. Root learned that one of the younger members had taken a golf-ball over the right eye and was being stitched up in the infirmary. Another had a painful bruise on the ankle but was continuing with the help of a volunteer who propped him up as he swung; Church thought it was against the rules, but he was shouted down. Someone had broken a window in trying to heft a four-iron shot over the clubhouse. His ball hadn't come down from the roof. Des Purseglove had reached the first tee in seven. Dr Fordham had made the halfway stage in twenty-eight. He had lost four balls and he was fuming.

Root kept out of his way. He told himself that he must drink no more, for he had Fordham's anecdote to repeat to Mabbatt.

He called Lecky away from Parsons, who was asking him his opinion of the greens. Jack Lecky was going to be a popular member.

Just as he was about to push a wristy shot that would take him a few yards further, if he should get out of the bunker, Sergeant Strapp came crunching along the gravel.

'Constable Root!' he called. 'I'm afraid I'll have to ask you inside – sorry!'

He mopped his sweating forehead. He looked hot and uncomfortable in his heavy sports jacket. Root automatically began to curse Strapp as he would anyone that interrupted his golf; he realized at once that his part in the Irish match was at an end. He recognized, however, that Strapp had tried to make it easy for him. Mabbatt would have bawled 'Root!' as if he were some kind of club servant at Wolvers Hall. He'd not forget to put in a good word for Strapp when the time came for him to send for an application for membership.

Parsons said to Lecky:

'Why don't you finish the round for him – you can't win, not officially. But you might as well have a knock.'

'And 'ave a drink, lad!' bawled Aspinall into his ear.

Lecky drank and agreed. Why not? It was turning out to be a perfect day. Elaine winked slyly at him.

'Sorry about your golf,' said Strapp.

'I wasn't in the running. I was bunkered for nine.'

'There's no rest on this job, not with CID,' said Strapp.

'He's still keen on Frank Bell?'

Strapp wiped more sweat from his face.

'He'd like to charge him. But there's nothing to pin it on him yet. Apart from the golf-ball. There's something new you don't know about.'

In spite of the heat, Root felt a cold sensation about the dampness of his spine. *Margaret*! How could she face it?

'Go on?'

'It's this maggot farm. Robinson was holding out.'

'The solicitor?'

'Him.'

'And?'

'It's worth a bit more than ten thousand. Turns out that they're building a motorway slap through it.'

128

Root struggled with his notions of compulsory purchase orders and planning permission.

'It takes the value up?'

'And how! It isn't just the motorway – it's the ideal spot for a service area. You know, caffs, restaurants, you name it, it's going to be there.'

'How much?'

'A hundred thousand. And upwards.'

'Jenny Piggott?'

Strapp shrugged. 'I could do with a beer. But I don't suppose I'll get a chance.'

'I'll get you one. Is she in it?'

'If she is, Mabbatt's the man to find out.'

Root withheld his doubts.

Twenty-one

' "Advice" is any counsel or suggestion which could influence a player ... Information on the Rules or Local Rules is not advice.'

Mabbatt was in his shirt-sleeves. His gaze was on a young uniformed officer who was trying to unroll a new map of the course. He had difficulty in driving the drawing pins into the oak panel behind the Secretary's desk.

'Use Sellotape,' Strapp told the anxious constable.

'Thanks, Sergeant.'

Mabbatt turned his gaze towards Root. It was like having a twenty-five pounder aimed at you. The morning's interview with the Chief Constable must have gone badly.

'You go now,' Mabbatt told the constable. 'Leave it to Sergeant Strapp.'

The young man went gratefully. Mabbatt kept his little eyes on Root.

'Well?'

It was a daily inquisition.

'Church behaves just as he always does, sir. He's his normal self now. That is, he's anxious and niggling as usual.'

'Parsons?'

'He's filling in time to the end of the month. He doesn't want to cause any more trouble. Just now I thought he'd have a row with Mr Church, but he held back.'

'Aye,' Mabbatt grunted.

'Then there's young Bell, sir. He's more himself too.'

Margaret had told Ursula about the results of the tests on the new golf-ball. The glass technologist had confirmed that it showed up at least twenty-five per cent more than any other. 'His young woman's been around to see my wife a couple of times; she usually does in the week. I was in the last time, late Friday night.'

He toned down the girl's indignant denunciation of the way that Frank had been interviewed night after night. Root could visualize her face. Young people always looked afraid when they complained about authority: the it's-not-fair look, Root called it in his own children.

'She's talking about writing to her MP, sir,' Root finished. 'She's standing by him. Wants him to patent the new paint he and his friend have worked out. He will, too. Seems it's marketable. She sees it as a sort of gesture against us, sir.'

Root knew, from Strapp, that Mabbatt had contemplated having Frank's house searched for the missing weapon; only his knowledge of Frank's intelligence had stopped him. A murderer would long since have got rid of the golf-club.

'He's a deep one, that,' said Mabbatt.

Root hurried on:

'Charlie Bliss looked a bit sick last night. He's recovered from his beating. I think Elaine's keeping him happy.'

Mabbatt probably knew about the developing liaison between Elaine and Lecky. No need to say anything about it.

'It's money!' growled Mabbatt. 'Money's in it. One of them's tied up with Tyzack's fancy woman – the one out at Thurlby. Who is it?'

Root tried to keep immobile. He had contributed nothing of value.

If he kept still, at least he wouldn't be a distraction to the others. Mabbatt looked at the new map. He put his big hand on the bright little figures in the spinney. Then he growled:

'It's too bloody convenient! He buys the farm and the land six months ago. Then he leaves it to his fancy piece and someone kills him. She must know something about it!'

'Would you like me to see her again, sir?' Strapp asked.

'No. I'll go. See if she's at home. I can be there and back before Root's pals start their dancing.'

'Before you go, sir, I've a bit of information,' said Root.

'Well?'

'It's about the old club-head we found on Monday. Dr Fordham knows whose it was – someone threw it at a rabbit years ago.'

'Threw it at what?'

'A rabbit, sir. It ran on to the green when they were putting. In nineteen twenty-seven. Dr Fordham was there.'

Mabbatt's huge purple-red face split into a smile.

'Well, bugger me,' he said slowly. 'Now I know it's a mad game! Throwing a golf stick at a bloody rabbit!'

'Shall I show PC Root the new search areas, sir?' asked Strapp.

'Let Bickerdike do it. You come with me. Root – go through these notes. Check the areas marked on the map. I want every inch of the grounds and the house searched again. Someone can't just have walked off with the stick. I want it found!'

The Superintendent left with Sergeant Strapp. He seemed unusually impatient to be away. This Piggott woman had got under his skin. Two of a kind, thought Root, who had come across the woman in her petrol attendant days. She had always been one to argue with the more obstreperous customers.

He crossed to the map and was studying it when Bickerdike entered the office with a sheaf of paper.

'Read these,' Bickerdike said shortly. 'He wants to know if you can think of any other possible search areas. We're using Army detectors.'

Root shook his head. He wished he had showered and changed his shirt. He began to read, slowly and carefully. After a while, Bickerdike left him.

It was a comprehensive plan. Nothing would be left to chance. The army's metal-detectors were superior affairs, more highly-tuned, more searching. Where there was a possibility that an underground drainage pipe might deceive the detectors, a hole would be dug. Two long drainage ditches would again be investigated. The pond that lay between the second green and the fourth tee would be pumped dry and the mud bulldozed out to a depth of ten feet. How many golf-balls would be found? He himself had put a dozen into its green-black water. Root put down his acquisitive inclinations. If he didn't make some kind of useful comment on the plan, he would probably be adjudged useless and returned to village bobbying. He reminded himself that he had decided to find Williamson, but now he was glad the scrounger had kept away from Wolvers. CID work was a specialized business. They wouldn't take kindly to his interference. An hour later, he sought out Bickerdike.

'It's good,' he told the Geordie. 'The only thing I'd add is that we haven't taken in as much of the old Hall as we could. I know metal-detectors wouldn't be any use. Too much iron in the building. But we could check the roof. Not that anyone could pitch a club up there. But someone could have gained access to it – maybe stuffed it down one of the chimneys.'

'Anything else?'

'There's the cellars. Mostly, they're blocked off, but someone could have forced a way through an exterior grill and shoved the club through.'

Bickerdike made a note. He saw that Root was hot.

'Had enough of us? Want to get back, do you, man?'

'There's nothing like your own cabbage-patch.'

'I wouldn't fancy yours.'

'Each to his own.'

Bickerdike stopped him as he was going:

'Hear about Church?'

'No. What about him?'

'I saw him twice this week. First time, his wife was there. Second time, he wasn't having it! Not him. Proper shirty. He said the next time I came he'd have his solicitor along, and I must make an appointment through his secretary. Well, Mabbatt said to go ahead, and I had this tight-lipped sod of a solicitor ripping me into pieces whatever I said. "I can't see that this is relevant" he'd say every time I got on to that randy stewardess of yours — shut me up sharp! I think his wife had a go at him after the first time I saw him. Doesn't like the idea of her husband being mixed up in the case of a murdered golfer. She's seen the pictures in the paper, and she's heard a whisper, if I know anything. Still, he did help.'

'How?' asked Root.

'He said he'd communicate some information through his solicitor so that it would be privileged.'

'Jenny Piggott?'

'In a way. Keep it under your hat.'

'I will.'

'Church heard about the motorway project and put two and two together, It's all at the secret stage in London, but these top men hear things. Between what he heard and what he guessed he knew the route that's been decided.'

'That's how Mabbatt found out about the maggot farm?'

'From Church.'

'A hundred thousand, Sergeant Strapp said.'

'More.'

'It's a lot of money. But Phil Church has plenty.'

'It isn't him that gains.'

'Who does?'

'Jenny Piggott.'

Root thought Mabbatt had been lucky.

'And Robinson knew about it too?'

Bickerdike looked down his long nose.

'He says he didn't.'

'He was a warm one!' Root said suddenly.

'Robinson?'

'Tom. Tom Tyzack!'

'Too clever,' said Bickerdike. 'He got himself killed, didn't he?'

Root went for his shower. He found a dozen or so more or less inebriated golfers throwing water at one another as they romped naked like so many over-sized cherubs. Charlie Bliss entered the steaming room with a tray of pints of beer. Root took one. There no rules on Captain's Day.

'Well you bugger!' bawled Aspinall. ' 'Ere's someone else pinching me drink!'

'More!' called Tufnell. 'Another ten pints!'

It seemed that the ghost of Tom Tyzack had been laid.

'Who won?' Root asked a bright pink figure.

'Won what?'

It was Phil Church. He was almost unrecognizable as the magnate who controlled the destinies of a large rolling-mill or as the fairly inept Secretary of Wolvers: his face was covered with lather, and his bristly white hair stiff with soap.

'Who won the match?'

Aspinall clutched Root's elbow.

' 'E wouldn't know – 'e didn't finish, did you, Churchie, lad! Lost your ball and 'adn't another with you! I'll tell you who won.'

Church held out his hands to search for the hot curtain of water.

'I know who won! Des Purseglove! Des won! Is that you, Arthur?'

'Yes.'

'Then point me to the water! I've got soap up my nose. Get out of the way!' he yelled to Aspinall, who was trying to pour beer down his neck. 'Ouch!'

'Couldn't organize a piss-up in a brewery!' bawled Aspinall. 'Come on, Churchie, this way!'

Between them Root and Aspinall guided Church to the water. The man was beside himself with rage.

'What's it coming to, when you can be insulted in the showers! Get off!' he squealed as Aspinall assaulted him with a stiff backed-brush.

It was the signal for half-a-dozen gleeful middle-aged men to remember their childhood. They rushed for cold water in their empty pint pots; they pelted Church unmercifully, tears streaming from

135

their eyes at the sight of the fat little haughty figure, and the sound of his indignation.

'Arthur! Do they always do this?' called Jack Lecky.

He was fully dressed. Clearly he and the others with him had been attracted by the uproar in the showers; the prancing, naked figure of Aspinall appeared with a glass of cold water. He took one bleared look at them and bawled:

'Get them!'

Cold water took Lecky in the face. His companions yelled with renewed glee. Root felt himself swaying with the effort of holding in his sides; he yelled with pain and laughter as the naked golfers pursued Jack Lecky and the others out into the corridor that led to the bar.

'Back! Back, you mad bastards!' someone shouted to them. 'Gentlemen! Bastards!'

They returned to the showers boasting and howling. Root considered it to have been the best Irish match of all.

'Poor old Tom should 'ave been 'ere!' called Aspinall. ' 'E were allus one for a bit of fun!'

Tufnell and the others agreed. Church was forgotten.

'Remember when he lost the keys to his car?' Tufnell said. 'Ah, Tom! Smashed every window in it, he were so mad!'

Root left them. It was time to go to the bar to wait for Ursula. As he dressed, he thought of Margaret Hughes. He wondered if she and Frank would turn up for the dance. More than likely Frank would want to stay at home, but Margaret was not one to hide in times of adversity. Fancy her making Frank patent the reflector paint! Root's own younger girl, Beth, had the same kind of sturdy will: straight as a die, she would stare him out if she was convinced that she was in the right. He always took her word. Instinct told him that he should take Margaret's about Frank: Frank couldn't kill.

He hoped Mabbatt would think so.

Twenty-two

'The competitor who holes the stipulated round or rounds in the fewest strokes is the winner.'

By nine o'clock carloads of wives, daughters, mistresses, aunties, and a mother-in-law or two were arriving. The members of Wolvers received them in the bar. Pretty young women were greeted rapturously by husbands, enviously by friends with less decorative women. The fashion in dresses that year in South Yorkshire ran mainly to prints: barbaric to Root's eye, they certainly added splashes of glaring colour to the dark oak panelling of the immense lounge-bar. Peacock blues and greens sprinkled with bright orange flashes: violent reds and blues with splatterings of pink and white: the men were drab by comparison. Most wore ancient, double-breasted evening suits that had seen twenty or thirty years of Masonic dinners, Rotary lunches, Club Dinners and the occasional boxing match. Church, who had learned about tropical wear, wore an immaculate white jacket; his wife had him firmly by the arm. One or two of the young bloods had frilled shirts and narrow trousers.

Root had bought his own suit second-hand from Moss Brothers. He knew he looked well. His wide shoulders and slim frame gave him an athletic appearance amongst generally over-fed club members.

'Arthur!' called two or three men from near the door. 'PC Plod! You've been caught – she's here!'

It was all said in the ribald tones of friends. Root squared his shoulders. His wife would be waiting in the vast lobby. He knew many men who envied him his wife – he could accept the envy, for he knew her to be a magnificent woman, just as she had been a fine-looking young girl.

'Hurry up!' called Elaine Bliss. 'Don't keep her waiting, Arthur!'

He smiled at her.

'Just going, Elaine.'

They were looking at one of the dim portraits in the lobby. Ursula in her long, trailing dress, the one that had meant so much saving for five years ago; Margaret Hughes in an African print that set off her tanned skin and elegant figure; and Frank Bell.

'Hello, Arthur,' said Ursula.

Root felt himself smiling a wide, foolish smile, just as he always did when he met his wife. She inspected him. Root knew that she was satisfied. She had early made him aware that he should dress well, at least as well as he was able to afford, if only to match her own splendid physical appearance. He knew that she admired him, and he gloried in the knowledge.

'I thought we'd all come together,' she said to him. 'I'll take Margaret out to the cloakroom. I suppose you'll want to get Frank a drink straight away? You haven't had a lot, have you?'

'I haven't,' he said. 'Come on, Frank – let's go in.'

More and more women were arriving. The lounge-bar was very noisy, whilst in the adjoining ladies' lounge a small dance-band was tuning up. Root heard the hollow thump of a drum and the whine of a violin. The same band had played at the Captain's Dance for the past thirty years.

Most of the men were discussing the day's match. How Aspinall had jumped into the pond to try to find a lost ball. Where Harry

138

Tufnell had tripped for the last time before abandoning the game. A difficult shot over the heads of a group in front that wouldn't give way. This or that incredible shot that had hit a tree, pitched on to the green and finished three inches from the bunker. A putt from off the green that had shot to the hole – never looked like doing anything else – and dropped. A drive with a six-iron that had gone as far as a two-wood could ever have done. And then the modest and immodest boasting.

Root began telling Frank about his own interrupted game, but Lecky rolled towards them in the middle of the account.

'Let you down, Arthur!' he said. 'Hello, Frank! How's your beautiful fiancée? Haven't you brought her?'

'She's here,' said Frank.

'Are they still pestering you?'

'Who?'

Root listened to the exchange unhappily.

'The rozzers!'

'Who says they're bothering me?'

Lecky, full of booze and sympathy, was momentarily puzzled by the unfriendly tone of Frank's voice. He stared owlishly at him.

'Everyone! Common knowledge, old lad – don't let them grind you down! Eh, Arthur? Oh, Christ, you are one!'

'Leave it,' said Root. 'Forget it,' he told Frank. 'Listen, both of you. This is a dance, not a police station. I know how you're suffering, Frank, and I know Jack here's trying to sympathize. But let it drop, both of you! Margaret's coming soon. So is my wife. And I don't want either of them upset!'

Frank's dejected face changed to a look of guilt.

'I'm sorry.'

'Didn't mean to butt in! I mean, no offence, Frank?' asked Lecky. 'I mean, we all know you didn't do it . . .'

'Drop it!' ordered Root.

Lecky grinned, sure of forgiveness with a drunk's certitude.

'How do you think Elaine's looking tonight?' he said.

Root looked again. Elaine looked quite delicious. Not an Ursula, of course, but a honey in her own right. Well-fleshed, the bosom soft

139

and cream-brown against the violent colours of her new dress, she radiated ripeness and enjoyment. Her arms were bare. Root's methodical inspection, product of twenty years of self-training, picked out a new-looking bangle on her arm. She intercepted his gaze. Involuntarily she transferred her glance to Jack Lecky.

Root smiled at her:

'She's a lovely girl.'

He ordered quickly to cover her embarrassment. The bracelet could have been solid gold. It had that dull, expensive sheen that made Denise Steel's ornaments the envy of the members' wives.

'You did want gin, didn't you, love?' he asked Margaret.

'I'm a big girl now, Uncle Arthur!'

'I keep forgetting.'

'Frank and I are going to be married soon,' she announced. 'I'm fed up of waiting. Frank is too.'

'Waiting does no one any good,' said Elaine Bliss.

Lecky winked at her to show her that he understood.

Ursula Root drank her vodka off quickly.

'Is that all we're getting before the dance, Arthur? I'm not driving back, you know. Frank is. He's the unlucky one this time. When is the band going to start? Though I suppose none of the men will want to leave. Do you know,' she said to Margaret, 'last year I had to drag him away from the bar – he won the prize, you know. It only amounted to a dozen golf-balls, but you'd have thought he'd won the Open. I couldn't get him away – he played every shot through twice over. I got so fed up I told him if he wanted to walk over the course once more, he'd better get his spikes on!'

Frank began to lose his frightened, constrained air. They must have given him a rough time, thought Root. Naturally, Bickerdike hadn't discussed it with him. But Root could imagine the endless questions, the bland, polite insinuations, the gentle reminders of tiny discrepancies between one night's answer and another's. Now, however, he was beginning to look like a young man who was in the company of his friends with the woman he loved.

'I didn't see you out today,' said Root carefully. 'You didn't want to play, Frank?'

'We were busy,' said Margaret loudly. 'We went to look at some houses, didn't we, Frank?'

Jack Lecky ordered more drinks. He patted Elaine's hand when she offered the change. Their mutual delight in touching one another was felt by the two couples near them: Ursula Root smiled indulgently. Even Frank Bell grinned at the unashamed lustfulness in Elaine's large eyes.

'You might as well tell us about the game,' said Ursula to Root and Lecky. 'It was a joint effort, wasn't it?'

Root told his part of the story, and Lecky demonstrated the further twenty-three shots that had taken him to the fourth green. All about the room, the same kind of discussion raged. Women began to form little counter-groupings of their own. But there was a wariness and a determination about them that suggested a refusal to be bypassed completely: a group gathered around Mrs Church like NCOs around a sergeant-major. When the elderly bandsmen struck up with the Gay Gordons to signal the start of the Dance, they would haul their husbands, lovers and fiancées into the ladies' lounge. First, however, there was the presentation.

Harry Tufnell had made a splendid recovery. He was dressed in a smart suit of impeccable cut. His shirt gleamed, and his tie was arranged with exactitude. Though he swayed very slightly, as though a ten-mile wind drifted through the smoky bar-lounge to lever him from side to side, he looked what he was, a successful car salesman. His speech was barely audible. Root heard some of it:

'I'm greatly honoured ... me, Harry Tufnell ... delighted ... drink with anybody here ... the noblest and the most ancient of all pastimes ... I give you ... Golf – '

'It's the presentation, Harry!' two or three of the members bawled. 'It isn't the dinner tonight!'

Tufnell must have mistaken the assembly for the Annual Club Dinner, when the Captain's principal toast, after the Queen, was to Golf.

' – a most notable pastime ... I didn't have a particularly good game ... missed the ball altogether once – '

The next words were lost in the storm of laughter and ribald

141

comments. Tufnell spoke on agreeably.

'. . . don't know how I did it . . . I do know that . . . splendid game . . . splendid player . . . er . . . er – '

He looked round not so much confused as politely interested in obtaining a true record.

'Des Purseglove!' Church called at his wife's prompting. 'Mr Desmond Purseglove won the prize!'

'. . . give you the winner of the Captain's Trophy . . . friend and fellow-golfer, Des Purseglove!'

Jack Lecky nodded, 'If I hadn't seen him come in on the fourth, I wouldn't have believed it,' he told Elaine Bliss.

'Who, love?'

His words were drowned in the storm of applause as Des Purseglove came to collect a small returnable statue of a golfer and the box of Penfold 'Ace' golf-balls.

'Him!'

Lecky whispered in a slurred voice again:

'Him! Thought he'd lost his ball and gone into the woods after it!'

Elaine lifted her glass to Lecky.

'Us?'

'Us!' Lecky repeated.

Purseglove made a short speech of thanks. He would have returned to his party, but Harry Tufnell stopped him.

'Marvellous performance – great golf, Des! Only wish another of . . . hup! . . . poor Tom could have seen it!'

Purseglove nodded. Everyone was staring at the two men in a kind of maudlin wonder.

'Aye, Tom!' growled a voice. 'Poor old Tom!'

'We'll have a drink . . . Tom!' Tufnell called.

The Captain had captured the imagination of the members. Solemnly they lifted their glasses and drank to the memory of Tom Tyzack. Aspinall somewhat spoiled the effect by charging to the bar and calling for a drink.

'Must – *must* drink to poor old Tom! Poor old sod!'

The moment was gone, and the conversation began again. Tom Tyzack's name was on all lips. Root knew he should be listening

142

now: waiting, analysing, searching the fabric of the many slurred discussions for a hint of something that could lead to the reasons behind Tom Tyzack's killing. He saw that Frank Bell had gone white. Margaret was keeping a discussion on house prices going: Ursula supported it well, but Frank could barely answer. Jack Lecky was going from the innocent-drunk to the happy-drunk stage.

Elaine Bliss gazed fondly at Lecky. She knew that she looked stunning; she realized that several members had noticed the way that Jack pressed her hand and stared for seconds at a time in that peculiarly aware manner that exists for lovers. What did it matter? Charlie, she realized, was what in South Yorkshire people described as a nowt man. He wanted a nowt job and a nowt way of life. Nowt in the way of children, nowt in the way of a home of his own, nowt in the way of work. He had always been a passenger. She had been the force in the marriage − the one who found the job that he could tolerate, the one who had to keep the job once it was found. You could, she said to herself, do a lot better. And if Jack could understand about the Committee-men, as he did, then she would take her chance with him. If he asked her. And he would.

'Lager and lime!' someone said in her ear.

'Sorry, love?'

'I asked twice already. Lager and lime.'

'Sorry, Mr Purseglove.'

It would be nice to think there would be no more Churches and Pursegloves; no more Tyzacks. Lecky knew how to treat a girl. Elaine willed herself not to think of the painted tower.

'A lager and lime and three pints. Then two whiskies, one straight, one with American Dry.'

Purseglove was still flustered by the presentation.

'All right. You did well today, Mr Purseglove.'

Purseglove smiled at her. Prestige meant a good deal to him, and Elaine knew it.

'I didn't do so badly.'

'Especially when you lost your ball.'

'I didn't lose a ball.'

'In the woods. You went in the woods.'

Purseglove smiled at her.

'Not me, Elaine! Get a drink for yourself as well. We might as well all celebrate my win. Round in sixteen – that's one better than last year.'

Elaine began grouping the drinks, swiftly and neatly. 'That all, Mr Purseglove?'

'You look a real beauty tonight, Elaine! Did you get your drink?'

Elaine indicated a glass of Dubonnet.

'Thank you very much.'

'That's all right!'

He looked at her once more.

Elaine thought he looked annoyed.

'I'm sorry about thinking that.'

'No more to be said! Cheers, Elaine!'

Elaine raised her glass, but she found herself turning to where Jack Lecky was telling the old chestnut about the golfer's wedding plans.

'. . . so she rushes on to the first tee in her wedding dress and her bouquet, all tear-stained and trembling, and what does he tell her?'

Root knew, Ursula knew, Frank knew. Margaret said:

'What?'

' "I said only if it was raining!" '

She laughed, the others joining in politely.

'Then there was the one about the golfer who dropped dead,' began Lecky.

'I think we'll leave that one,' said Root.

Lecky thought about it.

'Jesus!'

That was when Root saw the great, gaunt Geordie shouldering his way carefully through the noisy crowds towards them. Bickerdike had on a travesty of an evening suit. It was an ancient rusty-black garment, creased and badly-fitting. It seemed that a silent raven was winging down to them. Margaret saw him too.

'Frank!' she whispered.

Ursula Root said loudly into the silence that seemed to shroud what had been a gay little group:

'You want to think about where you're going to stay, Margaret.

And you, Frank. The honeymoon!'

Frank Bell watched the progress of the policeman in horrified fascination. He could not take his eyes from the approaching black figure.

'They'll all be booked up until the end of September,' went on Ursula. 'How about Portugal, Frank?'

She moved to confront him.

'What about taking Margaret to Portugal on your honeymoon?'

Bickerdike had to wait for a few seconds whilst Aspinall got out of his way; he had a tray of whiskies on his head. To the yells of approval from his pals, he weaved an uncertain passage amongst the hilarious members and their thawing wives. There was always a story to tell about Aspinall the day after the Captain's Dance.

Margaret stood firm.

'I'd like Portugal,' she said. 'I've never been. When did you go, Ursula?'

'We haven't been,' Root heard his wife say. 'But we will one year, won't we, Arthur?'

'We will.'

But would Frank Bell be able to take Margaret Hughes there? Root's mind whirled as he reviewed the investigation. Was Frank in it? Mabbatt had left to interview Jenny Piggott. There could be a connection between her inheritance and one of the suspected men who had access to the death spinney. Frank? Computers? Information stored on a computer – something secret, something about the future of the motorway? Could Frank have gained access to vital plans and then made a compact with Jenny Piggott? Root shook his head.

The booze was affecting him now.

Trust to instinct, he said to himself. The face of his daughter, Beth, stiff with pride and resolve when unjustly treated, became the unrelenting proud face of Margaret Hughes talking honeymoon plans with his wife as Sergeant Bickerdike came up to them.

Bickerdike looked at Frank Bell: and then he turned to Root.

'Excuse me,' he said, realizing that the rest of the party was unashamedly staring at him. 'I'm sorry. It won't take long.'

He jerked his head to show that he wanted a private word with Root. They moved a pace or two away. No one else took any notice of them.

'Parsons,' Bickerdike said quietly. 'Find him and bring him to the Secretary's office.'

Parsons!

Root exerted himself to compose his features. He did not say the little professional's name aloud.

'Yes,' was all he replied.

The band struck up the Gay Gordons.

His wife looked a question. Frank Bell allowed whisky to slop down his shirt-front; Ursula took the glass.

'Why don't you take Margaret for a dance?' she said to Frank.

Still trembling, Frank Bell reached for Margaret.

'Yes! Yes.'

'May I have the honour, Mrs Root?' Lecky said, enunciating carefully. 'What a distinguished pair you look, by the way — if I'd been told you were a copper and his missus, I'd never have believed it!'

'There's nothing wrong with being a copper,' said Root.

'Nor his missus,' Ursula added.

'I believe you both!'

'And we will go to Portugal!' Margaret said over her shoulder. 'We will!'

Twenty-three

'A player who has incurred a penalty shall state the fact to his opponent . . .'

Parsons was dancing with Denise Steel. They made a vital, attractive pair. Parsons moved lightly for a heavily-built man; his feet flashed over the shining boards almost daintily. He was sweating, hugely enjoying himself in the old-fashioned dance. The band paused for a few seconds, and the beat became that of a lively march: the Military Two-Step. Denise Steel sprang to attention. Parsons did a mock curtsey, and the pair of them swept away just as Root was nearing them. She was almost the only woman to have disregarded the dictates of fashion. Instead of the African prints, she wore a white ball-dress all frills and flounces. Her heavy bosom bounced up and down and her diamonds flashed pin-points of sparks at the rest of the sedately-dancing women. Whatever she did, thought Root, she would defy convention. Some people made a career of it. Root grinned at that: his wife would have called it typical Yorkshire thinking.

The next time Parsons came near him, he moved quickly.

'Jack!'

'Arthur, lad! You excusing me — want a whirl with our Denise? Isn't she gorgeous!'

He joggled with Denise's bosom. She shrieked with laughter.

'Oh, stop it, you dirty dog! Isn't he terrible!'

The music came to a climax. Dancers held firmly to their partners, whirled six or seven times round and stopped, glad of the rest. Sunbrowned golfing faces beamed with pleasure. Wives patted their hair and worried about perspiration. Men and women fancied a drink. The Captain's Dance was a success.

'You're wanted, Jack — can I take him for five minutes, Mrs Steel?'

Denise Steel stopped giggling when she heard the request. 'Mrs Steel', Arthur had called her.

'Why, what's up?'

Jack Parsons hadn't spoken.

'Routine, Mrs Steel. I expect he'll be back soon.'

'Tom?' asked Parsons.

'I couldn't say,' Root lied. 'Ready, Jack?'

He realized that he was using his official voice, the one that coated an instruction with a sugaring of persuasive gentleness. It left no doubt about its intention, however. Parsons nodded.

'That Mabbatt?'

'Yes, the Superintendent.'

'He'd never make a golfer.'

Parsons was taking it calmly. He showed no sign of discomfiture.

'Don't get carried away by one of your fancy men while I'm gone,' he told Denise.

'Oh, Jack!'

'Right,' he said. 'Lead on, Arthur. Watched your swing the other afternoon, by the way. Friday. Not bad. You're going back nicely enough. Try to make it more of a sweep, though. You're hurrying it.'

Root was grateful for the advice. Perhaps that had been the trouble with the six-iron shot that afternoon, the one that had taken him into the sycamore copse. He flexed the muscles of his shoulders. Sweep. Sweep it away. No tension. The wrists easy and fluid. Was that the secret?

'Thanks, Jack.'

'Going to tell me what it's about?'

'I wouldn't if I knew. And I don't.'

'It is about Tom. Don't kid me, Arthur!'

'I wouldn't be surprised.'

'Aye.'

Mabbatt was pleased with himself.

'Mr Parsons!' he exclaimed, getting up ponderously from Church's chair. 'I wanted a word with you – you don't mind leaving the dance for a few minutes, do you?'

'I'll try not to let it bother me.'

Root wondered whether he should stay. Bickerdike pushed a chair forward for the professional. Root stood by the door. Mabbatt had been interviewing Jenny Piggott with Sergeant Strapp: would Mabbatt remember to tell him to go away? Root hoped he would not. When Bickerdike had been moving towards the little group in the bar-lounge, he had been aware of a certain elation in the gaunt Geordie's face: there was the same look of expectancy and faintly cruel pleasure on Mabbatt's wide, big-nosed countenance. Things were moving to a climax. The hunt was on. And Root wanted to be one of the pack once the cry was up.

Mabbatt hardly noticed the village bobby's presence. Root might as well have been another sooty oil-painting. Mabbatt felt the excitement of near-success. He knew that Parsons was a tough nut, but then he liked cracking tough nuts. This wouldn't be the only interrogation. Parsons was unlikely to give much away during half-a-dozen sessions of close questioning. But something would eventually come out. One slight evasion – one subtle twist of direction: and then Mabbatt would have a lever. One lie, Mabbatt promised himself. Even half a lie would do. And then he would have the conceited adulterous little bastard.

He savoured the coming moments.

A chance remark had started it out at Thurlby.

Jenny Piggott was expecting company, so much could be seen at a glance. The comfortable chairs were arranged neatly, cushions displayed to maximum advantage. There was a tray of drinks, tumblers, and a plastic tub – ice, surely, thought Mabbatt, feeling thirsty – on one table; and, symmetrically, another table with the sort of eatables that Mabbatt associated with the schoolmaster who had claimed his wife two years before. Little puff pastry cases with minced prawns and sickly mushroom fillings: food for pansies, not men.

Jenny was not pleased to see Mabbatt, though she managed a smile for Strapp.

'Will you be long?' she wanted to know once they were indoors. 'It's not I don't want to help, only I'm busy tonight.'

Mabbatt found himself becoming filled with sullen rage. She'd got another man. Straight away. No waiting. Like bloody rabbits. All the same, women. Here she was, stinking of gin and waiting to pump whisky into her next fancy man. He glared into her strange eyes. He found himself taking in her whole presence. She was a randy-looking piece. He began to hate the man she was expecting.

'I've just a few questions,' he began hoarsely. Then he cleared his throat. 'Questions concerning the murder of Thomas Geoffrey Tyzack.'

'I told you all I knew.'

She was almost apologetic. There was no sign of the hostility she had shown on Mabbatt's earlier visit.

'We've been looking into Mr Tyzack's affairs,' Mabbat told her.

Her gaze went to the drinks.

'Oh, yes?'

'We're interested in the bequest Mr Tyzack made to you, Miss Piggott.'

'He must have thought it were a joke!' she said half-nervously. 'I mean, a maggot farm!'

Strapp decided to say something:

'It's a valuable property, Miss Piggott.'

Mabbatt nodded. Strapp could sense the air of mutual curiosity between the huge Superintendent and the ripe woman. Could it be, he asked himself. Could it? Did old Mabbatt fancy her?

'I'm not complaining,' she said. 'Mr Robinson reckons I can live on the income. The couple that manage it want to stay on. And I'm not robbing her,' she said, pointing in the general direction of Wickinglow. 'Has she said anything?'

'Mrs Tyzack's very comfortably provided for,' Strapp told her.

'Well then.'

'Did you have any idea of the value of the property?'

The tone was peremptory. I'm wrong, Strapp told himself. The old bastard's not going soft after all.

'How could I? I didn't know Tom were leaving it me. He always said he'd be generous. I've money put by. And he said there'd always be a job if he went broke. Though he weren't likely to – he were too smart!'

She was proud of him, Strapp realized. She would always need a successful, bold man about her. Who were the drinks for?

'Expecting company?' Mabbatt snapped.

Jenny Piggott remembered now the insulting questions of Monday morning.

'What if I am?'

'I wouldn't want you to be kept waiting.'

Strapp saw Jenny Piggott become enraged too. There *was* something between them. Mutual distrust, hate, contempt, sexual attraction – it was like watching two children after a close friendship had gone wrong.

'Well, I won't be kept waiting then! Come on – what do you want?'

Mabbatt smiled, to Strapp's amazement.

'Mind if I sit down for a moment, Miss Piggott? It's been a long day. And I've been on my feet all day.'

Automatically she responded with the ready sympathy of one worker for another.

'I'll make some – ' she began.

'Thanks, Miss Piggott! Sit down, Sergeant. You don't mind if he sits down too?'

'No. No.'

She didn't know the way about this social occasion. Jenny Piggott couldn't decide whether to sit down herself, if so where to sit, what to

151

offer in the way of drinks, whether or not to smoke: and Mabbatt was simply sitting there looking at her. He made her feel wonderfully uncomfortable. He was too big even for the large, robust chairs. Big, menacing and too quiet by far.

Mabbatt waited.

'She hasn't been!' Jenny said at last. 'I thought she would! I went to see him buried. I know she wanted to speak but she didn't. I don't see why I shouldn't have gone. I liked Tom as much as her. I've nothing against her – it isn't for me to call her first, is it?'

Mabbatt deliberately scraped away at the bowl of his pipe. He didn't often smoke it, but Strapp had seen him use it as a stagey prop a score of times.

Jenny watched him. She waited for him to speak.

Strapp knew better than to break the silence. There was, he supposed, a technique in it, but if there was it consisted almost entirely of patience. Mabbatt knew the trick. Wait. Wait. Wait, and wait again. Keep the flow going until it dried up, then add a little leverage and it would start again. If there was anything there at all, eventually it would come out.

'What sort of thing did you want to know?' Jenny asked. Her previous question about the protocol for discussing Tom with Mrs Tyzack had been met only with a non-committal grunt and a further investigation of Mabbatt's black pipe.

In answer to this question, Mabbatt looked again into the wide, today almost green eyes and stared her down.

She went on hurriedly:

'I miss him. I never thought I would, but I do. I'd known him a long time. I were an attendant on the pumps. Did you know? I suppose I told you before. They called us petrol cowgirls. That was what he said. Cowgirls! It isn't really funny, but he had a way of making it sound funny. Who do you think did it?'

She sounded half-scared now. Strapp wondered if this was the time for Mabbatt to begin on the line of inquiry that had brought them from the golf course to this comfortable but rather warm room. He wished Jenny would offer them a drink. But she didn't know how to adapt socially. All she could do was to gabble.

'I hope you'll catch him. Tom weren't what you'd call a gentleman, but no one should have done that to him. They said in the paper his head were split open. It's awful! It really is! I knew him years ago before he started putting weight on. He were a fine figure of a man then! As broad as you, but not so tall.'

Jenny licked her lower lip. She had bright red lipstick thickly spread. She was as inviting as a jam butty to a hungry lad.

On she talked.

She told about her days in Sheffield as a go-go girl. It hadn't been much of a life, though the applause had been marvellous. You met too many dirty-minded middle-aged men, but she could understand how they felt now that she herself was getting on. It all seemed a long time ago. Then she couldn't do the dancing the same as she once could and the travelling disco owner had told her frankly that she'd had it, love, and he'd got a sixteen-year-old. And we all go off, love, don't we? Two weeks' wages, no job, no savings, no training for anything, and what could a girl do? She'd turned down a couple of offers vaguely presented as housekeeper or companion. And then it popped out, a bright nugget of information that had Mabbatt's eyes glittering like a pig seeing the trough magically refilled.

'I could've gone to Woollie's or one of the other chains, but I were going through the middle of Rotherham one day and who should I bump into but Jack Parsons, and we had a drink and I told him I was out of a job and he said there was a job going at the garage down the road and why didn't I go for it?'

Unaware of the effect she had produced, she went on:

'They wanted a smart girl, I don't suppose you'd have said I was a girl – I was all of twenty-seven. No. Twenty-eight. But I've always had good legs, even though I put a bit of weight on. And they wanted someone who'd been around and could chat the customers up a bit. Jack said the new owner wanted to get regular customers coming back, so we had to wear these red plastic boots winter and summer – not all the girls wanted a job dressing up like that, though nowadays they wouldn't care if they had to go topless!'

Mabbatt filled his pipe.

He listened to an account of Jenny's training, which had been brief enough. And then how the boss had taken a fancy to her, and how she'd told him what to do, only he kept on and eventually she said all right and here she was with a maggot farm.

'Would you like a drink?' she finished. 'Whisky?'

'Please.'

'How about your Sergeant?'

'The same, please, Miss.'

She couldn't detect the gleam of triumph in Mabbatt's eye, for he avoided looking at her directly. She felt that there was nothing more to say, that she had co-operated fully, bared her soul; and that they should go soon.

'You wouldn't be waiting for Jack now, I suppose?' Mabbatt said conversationally.

'Jack?'

The woman spoke politely.

'Jack Parsons.'

'Jack!'

'From the golf club.'

'Jack Parsons!'

'Parsons,' Mabbatt repeated. 'Mr Parsons is a friend of yours, isn't he?'

Jenny Piggott's slow mind began to adjust to the fact that there would be more questions, that her efforts to get rid of the two policemen had been unsuccessful, and that there was a positive hostility in Mabbatt's query. Yet now that she had given the big man a drink, she was reluctant to respond to her feelings.

'How did you know?' she said.

'You said so. He got a job for you. With Mr Tyzack.'

'He didn't!'

'You've just told me that he did.'

'But he didn't!'

'Miss Piggott, this is a murder investigation.'

'I know!'

'Then answer me!'

They enjoyed it, thought Strapp. They were both panting, just as before.

154

'He weren't a friend of mine – not since I worked in Sheffield!'

'You knew him well?'

'I knew lots of fellers! It were part of the job – you had to spend time with them!'

'But he introduced you to Mr Tyzack's employment.'

'No!'

'You've told me that he did.'

'I only said he told me there were a job going – I can get my own jobs, thank you!'

'What time do you expect him?'

'What!'

'Tonight.'

' 'E isn't coming! No! It isn't 'im! It's . . .'

She hesitated.

'Who?'

Strapp found himself tense with expectancy. Mabbatt's luck, he thought. Mabbatt, with his massive patience, had stumbled on it. Was it luck, though? The connection existed – all Mabbatt had done was to sit through the words until there was a reference that corresponded to the pattern of events. Parsons. Jenny Piggott. Tyzack. And a piece of land that might easily be worth a quarter of a million pounds. If Church was any judge.

'Who's coming tonight?' asked Mabbatt.

'Not Jack Parsons! I never went with 'im. I never fancied 'im! Tom would have made three of little clever Jack Parsons – he were only out for himself!'

That was true enough, thought Strapp. But it merely reinforced what they knew. Parsons was out of golf, his livelihood. He could exist only on what Denise Steel chose to push his way. The problem was to prove a connection, a continuing one, between Jenny Piggott and Parsons, and to find the link between the professional and the secret of the motorway. It was a good deal less fanciful than a murder committed for the secret of extra-luminous golf-balls.

Mabbatt gave up very quickly after that.

'You won't get in touch with Mr Parsons, will you, Miss Piggott?' he ordered.

155

Strapp thought he was going out on a limb, but it was a chance worth taking. The woman watched them go with bewildered fury in her expression. She made as if to clear away the glasses the policemen had used; but she stopped and saw them to the door.

'I never saw Jack in six years!' she called after Mabbatt.

'Good night, Miss Piggott!' he answered.

He was smiling as they returned to Wolvers.

Strapp saw that the smile had not worn off. Root, standing by the door, looked apprehensive at this show of pleasantness. He'd never make a detective, thought Strapp. But he was a bloody good golfer. Strapp mentally went through the basic elements of Root's short backswing. He got a tremendous acceleration from a point about fifteen inches behind the ball. He had good wrists, boney, but powerful. And his hands were strong. Comes of trying lock-ups, Strapp smiled to himself, thinking of long night-beats. No more of those!

'Now, Mr Parsons!' began Mabbatt. 'Where did you find out the true value of the maggot farm?'

Twenty-four

'Any movable obstruction may be removed . . .'

Jack Lecky was the first to reach the painted tower. Moonlight filtered through the mock slits. Some of the glass was gone. Impulse made Lecky look out on to the grey-blackness of the golf course. He could make out the groups of sombre trees as the top branches swished about in the light wind. Beyond the course was the road to Sheffield, busy with the traffic of mad hour – the rush home when the pubs closed. Yellow sodium lights made a string of irregular beads through a heavy growth of beech trees along the eleventh fairway. In the immediate foreground was the spinney where Tyzack had been murdered.

Lecky shivered. He could hear the death-cry again.

He made himself think of Elaine Bliss's rounded charms.

An ordinary working-girl, he told himself. Just what I need. No clever conversation over the breakfast-table about the swinging people poor Pat had read about in the glossies; no agonizing about women becoming vegetables; no endless, dreary discussions about the headmaster Pat worked for who was standing against the rising tide of revolutionary youth by not allowing the prefects to smoke in their common-room. Where was Pat now?

He chuckled.

He need never again listen to the brainless chatter of a clever woman.

'Jack!'

Lecky turned, started.

Elaine Bliss stood in a shaft of moonlight. The weird colouring of her dress made her seem almost a painted figure, like those faded creatures commissioned by a coal magnate a century and a half before. The white of her eyes was a startling brightness. Her dark hair glistened silkily. Her swelling breasts heaved.

'I ran all the way – I'm puffed, Jack!'

He laughed aloud. The tower rang with the noise.

Faintly, from far below, the heavy beat of a tango filtered through heavy floors and massive walls.

'You and me, Elaine,' he said. 'Just us!'

Then they made love.

Two floors below, in the Secretary's office, Parsons was bellowing with laughter. When he stopped for a moment, he said:

'A what farm!'

'A maggot farm. Maggot.'

'You're having me on!'

Mabbatt got to his feet.

'I want to know about your connection with the Piggott woman,' he said. 'Everything.'

Parsons began to laugh again. Then he stopped.

He too got to his feet.

'You're not having me on, are you.'

It wasn't a question.

'Piggott woman – do you mean Jenny Piggott?'

'Her.'

Strapp put in:

158

'We've got her statement here, Mr Parsons. We know about you and her.'

Parsons' quick temper flared up.

'And what's that supposed to bloody well mean!'

'You tell me,' said Mabbatt.

Menace, thought Root. Sheer physical menace. The good big guy against the small bad guy. Force the evil to the surface by fright.

What if there was no evil?

'This is the Captain's Dance!'

'Yes,' agreed Mabbatt.

His body relaxed as the professional sat down.

'I've got company – can't it keep until morning?'

'It's important Mr Parsons. Murder is always important.'

There was a pause.

Root remembered what Strapp had once told him: Mabbatt used silence as well as he used the anger which he could turn on so readily. All at once he thought of Syd Smethurst's lad. What was Hunt making of him? He himself had been quiet with the distraught youth. Not said much. Waited – listened for the sobbing break in the boys' breathing and then heard about the trouble. All youth's trouble. Parents at a distance. Schoolmasters who didn't want to know you if you were not too bright and big for fourteen.

But Parsons had patience too.

He was good with crowds, Root recalled. When the pressure was on in a tournament, Parsons could be relied on to keep his nerve. A three-foot putt was a three-foot putt whether two hundred assorted spectators held their breath as you took it or not: mostly, the putts went in. If only his play through the green was as good as his driving and his putting, Parsons would be in the big time. But he just hadn't got the consistency to set his iron shots down one after another like poached eggs. A pity.

His patience might be of use to him, though, if he were sent down for life.

'Jenny Piggott!' snapped Mabbatt.

Parsons answered at once:

'She were only a bloody club girl! Wasn't she a go-go girl?'

Ursula Root was dancing with a man she disliked. She wasn't sure of his name, but he insisted on dancing with her at every Captain's Dance. He was a charming little man with bad breath and a habit of calling her 'my dear'.

'Ursula, my dear, we don't see enough of you! Why not get Arthur to bring you along at the weekend? He's always here – surely you can be spared from the kitchen sink for an hour or two?'

Ursula wondered whether to walk off. She wanted to tell him that a police-constable's pay might run to the odd pint for Arthur, but not to vodkas for her as well. And she didn't particularly like the atmosphere of the club at weekends anyway. Not with silly little men like him paying compliments but not daring to do or say more.

She allowed herself to be whirled around. And she managed to smile, especially when she saw that Frank Bell and Margaret Hughes had their arms round each other and were making for the door that led to the lobby. Two weeks in Portugal! Lucky them!

She wondered where Arthur was.

'Folks keep disappearing!' her partner said. 'Expect they're finding it hot in here. I do, I know!'

Ursula asked him if he had played in the match.

'No! Not me – can't say as I'd enjoy it. Not being a good player, like your husband. Why has he left you all alone, my dear?'

Ursula deliberately tripped him. He recovered at once.

'Whoops! My fault, my dear!'

The band sawed, thrummed and banged into a crescendo. 'The Blue Tango' echoed around the vault-like ceiling, shaking the electric chandeliers and the heavy velvet drapes. Perspiring golfers complained to their wives. Wives smiled and flexed their muscles. Charlie Bliss danced with one of the bar-maids, and no one took exception. Aspinall went out to be sick. The Captain's Dance wasn't just a success: it was a triumph.

'My divorce,' Lecky said. 'Listen.'

'I must look a sight! I'll have to get some make-up on before we go down!'

'We're not going down yet.'

160

Elaine clung to Jack Lecky.

'Aren't we?'

'No. Listen, love. I'm half-stoned I know. I'm someone you met a week ago. I don't *care* about anything you've done before – it isn't anything at all!'

Elaine waited. She smoothed the new dress that still smelt of new stuff and the residual traces of dyes. In the bright moonlight Jack's handsome, experienced face looked sharper, bolder. What would poor chubby Charlie make of him when he found out! She was trembling.

'I should go down.'

'It's stuffy in here.'

They stared at one another.

'We could go up on to the roof,' Elaine said. 'But I have to go down soon. I'll be missed.'

'Which way?'

'There. The door's stiff, but they go through this way to fix the telly aerials.'

Lecky found the massive iron handle. It might be easier to talk in the fresh air. There was a stiffish breeze. Just what he needed to blow the cobwebs away.

On the dusty stairway they held one another for a full five minutes.

The bandsmen pointedly made the crescendo louder and longer than any before. Their leader bowed to the dancers and closed the lid of the grand piano. Without undue haste, the band made as one man for the rear of the bar where, by arrangement, Charlie Bliss had a tray of pint pots waiting. The Captain paid for all they could drink. And Harry Tufnell was no piker.

Outside, Margaret Hughes was holding Frank Bell's head against her breast. She tried to talk about the coming honeymoon, but he was shivering with emotion. The constant interrogating had upset him more than she had realized. For all his solid build and his native Yorkshire confidence, the prospect of imminent arrest had undermined his whole personality. She felt a surge of anger against the unknown killer, for whoever he was he had taken more than Tyzack's life.

'Frank!' she whispered urgently. 'Frank!'

Eventually he responded. He seized her powerfully and she moulded her splendid body against him.

He spoke in a low voice:

'That day – Sunday. I thought you believed it was me. That's why I was so mad at Charlie Bliss. It wasn't him at all.'

'Oh, Frank! How daft can you be!'

Surely he must know that she *knew* him! Always had! Margaret embraced him with an ecstasy of reassurance.

'What was she like?' asked Elaine Bliss.

'I told you before. Nothing like you.'

'She was a schoolteacher, wasn't she?'

Lecky could laugh at the memory of his wife's pride in her professional standing.

'A graduate too. Very clever.'

'I'm not clever.'

Jack Lecky felt himself sobering fast. He had his arm around Elaine's shoulders. The wind was quite strong up here on the roof. He put out a hand to one of the stone battlements. It flaked in his hand. He remembered someone telling him that parts of the stonework had weathered badly.

'You know, this is mad,' he said. 'Up here on the roof – all those people down there, and they can't see us – me half-stoned, you not so far off: on top of a tower!'

'What's mad about it?'

'Nothing!'

'Well!'

Yet Lecky could sense that his own unspoken feelings were shared. Though she couldn't verbalize too well, Elaine felt. He was sure of that.

'The divorce could take months. I don't want to wait.'

She spoke very certainly.

'I *can't* wait.'

'You'll come?'

'As soon as you want me.'

162

'What about your husband?'

Elaine had thought about it.

'Charlie can look after himself.'

'Pack tonight.'

'Yes.'

Lecky looked over the course, and a sobering thought struck him: would his application be turned down, now that he was to take the stewardess away? He laughed at the idea. Elaine wanted to know why he was laughing.

'I was thinking – how do I stand with the stewardess at home! The Committee isn't going to like it!'

Elaine made a vulgar remark about the Committee. Pat could never have made the words sound so convincing. Lecky congratulated himself again.

They were standing very close to one another, both thinking about the future, when the moon slid behind a fast-moving cloud. Elaine began to think, quite inconsequentially, about curtains in a house of her own. Lecky wished he had saved some of the whisky.

Neither heard the soft footsteps behind them. Far below, the sound of a car starting up in the car-park at the back of the Hall covered the rush of the assailant.

Jack Lecky heard something. He turned his head a little and caught a glimpse of blackness against the horizon. Someone moving very fast. And then, nothing.

Elaine Bliss was petrified.

She was falling with Lecky, her hand still clutched in his as he collapsed against the rotten stone of the battlement. She wanted to say 'What did you do that for?' when she saw the face of the assailant.

Nothing came out. She was a tumbled heap of dark colours.

She tried to scream. She opened her mouth, but the force of a heavy blow knocked the breath from her body. She read murder in the man's eyes.

'No!' she gasped with what breath came to her, as he kicked her again.

She had enough strength to get to her feet. And that was, most terribly, the wrong thing to do.

Elaine Bliss looked down once at the face of Jack Lecky, who was lying in a pool of black liquid; and then she was hit twice savagely in the stomach.

Her half-turn towards the gap in the rotten stone was completed by the ruthless man behind her. She could see far down into the night. Below, a light from the men's locker-room showed the irregular flag-stones of the path between the flower beds.

She felt her legs taken. A searing pain filled her.

She screamed as the man hacked at her grip on the stonework. His face was the last thing she identified.

The killer turned to Jack Lecky.

Twenty-five

'If a player play when his partner should have played, his side shall lose the hole.'

Root's doubts about Mabbatt had not been resolved. Now, Mabbatt was making too much of a meal of interrogating the pro. He showed his enjoyment.

They had been over Parsons' statement twice. And yet, though Mabbatt had tried to browbeat him, Parsons had remained cool. One brief flash of anger had come of Mabbatt's questioning, but no more. Parsons hadn't liked a reference to the wife and children he had deserted, but he had regained control of himself. Mabbatt, thought Root, was sticking his neck out. More and more he disliked the notion of Parsons as murderer.

Half-an-hour went by. Still the questions went on. What did you say to Mrs Steel? Why did you go to look at the corpse? What did you say to Tyzack the last time you saw him before the Sunday in question? And why didn't you divulge your relationship with Jenny

165

Piggott earlier?

'Divulge it!'

Parsons had laughed.

'She was only a pick-up in the club! Club Maxime, that's what it was called – you could get any girl there! I used to go with my mates. Twice a week. But the bloody place closed down five years ago! You lot wouldn't let them keep on.'

Mabbatt knew. He himself had played some part in persuading the magistrates to refuse the club a licence. Too many villains used it. They'd be just Parsons' type. Clever buggers all.

Mabbatt was going to start from the beginning again when they heard the long, wailing scream. It was cut off by a dull, thumping sound.

Outside, Frank Bell and Margaret Hughes jumped apart in fright. Elaine Bliss lay ten yards from them in a patch of light from the locker-room. Her gay, peacock dress stirred as her broken limbs twitched. Then they were still.

Margaret began to scream.

Mabbatt was through the door before Root. Strapp rushed downstairs after them. They came across Frank Bell who was trying to stop Margaret's screams.

'Take her in!' snapped Root. 'Now!'

'The stewardess!' Mabbatt called.

'She's fallen!' Strapp said, looking up and seeing the battlements high above.

'Fallen!' Mabbatt snapped. 'Get up there – Root! Strapp! Quick!'

They raced grimly for the wide portico. Then they had to push their way through the milling crowd who wanted food and drink or a breath of fresh air or a chance to be alone with a lover.

'What's 'urry?' bawled a drunken Aspinall.

'I *beg* your pardon!' said a woman hastily placed to one side by Root's big hands.

Strapp followed as Root leapt up the marble stairs three at a time.

166

A startled waitress moved out of the way, spilling a tray of empty glasses as she did so. A couple entwined in one another's arms looked up, but Strapp had passed them.

Their pace did not slacken as they gained the second storey. Here, the stairs were narrower, meaner. There was mahogany nearly black with age, brass rails green with a hundred years of neglect. Dust lay thickly on the stairs. When they reached the tower, Root did not wait for the sergeant, though perhaps he should have done so in the interests of safety.

'Root! Wait!'

But already Root was impatiently thrusting aside the heavy door and stumbling into the narrow, winding staircase in the side of the tower. No one came down. He half-expected a furious onrush of some manic figure, desperate to escape.

He heard Strapp calling to him again, but he would not stop.

He hesitated when he picked out a dark shape near the edge of the battlements. Thin moonlight filtered through a light banking of cloud. From the woods came a vicious, snarling cry. A hunting cat, thought Root. Gone wild. The dark figure snorted, struggling for breath.

Root realized that whatever it was, it could not harm him. It was a victim, not an assailant.

He had to puzzle over the features for a few seconds before he recognized Jack Lecky.

Lecky had been jammed into a battlement. His face was covered with thick blood and flakes of rotten stone.

'Got him!' roared Strapp.

'It's Jack Lecky,' said Root. 'Get an ambulance. And the doctor—no! You wait here! I'll find Fordham quicker.'

Strapp asserted his authority.

'No!' he snapped, all sergeant. 'You wait. See that he can breathe!'

'Right, Sergeant.'

Strapp rushed away.

As he eased Lecky down onto the lead covering of the roof, Root could hear screams and shouts from below. Mabbatt's loud tones dominated all.

Lecky's eyes opened.

Even in the poor light Root could see the signs of shock and concussion. The sooner Jack was in hospital the better.

'Elaine?' Jack was trying to say.

Root thought of the heavy gold bangle on the broken and bleeding arm.

'Don't worry,' he said.

Lecky's eyes closed.

Root determined that Mabbatt would not be the one to tell him about the death of Elaine Bliss.

Twenty-six

'The player is entitled to relief from obstructions . . .'

Mabbatt organized the investigation with admirable efficiency. The machinery of a large force was set in motion at once. When the immediate matters were settled – Lecky on his way to hospital, Elaine Bliss confirmed as dead, an announcement was made to the shuffling, rather tipsy crowd, and instructions given as to where they might go until they were released.

Fordham was waiting with his report.

'Mrs Bliss died almost immediately after her fall, Superintendent. I'd have said immediately, had young Bell not told me she stirred. Though your pathologist might still find she died at once – her movements could have been reflex actions. Multiple injuries, shock, both would have been responsible for death. A nasty business.'

Mabbatt put away his frustration.

'And Mr Lecky, doctor? You could see something?'

'Only what I saw in the light of my torch. Enough to know that he needed to be hospitalized at once. Can't tell about fractures. Of the skull, I mean. He was concussed. One blow only, probably with something fairly heavy and smooth.'

'Not a golf-stick?'

Fordham did not smile at the false description.

'No. Not sharp-edged at all. And I'd say the handle of a golf-club would be too light. The usual blunt instrument, that's what he was hit with.'

'There's no chance that he could have inflicted the injury on himself?'

They both knew what the question meant. Strapp was glad that PC Root was out of the room.

'None. The injury is fairly high on the back of the head. Of course, your pathologist might disagree. Did you find a weapon?'

'Not yet, Doctor.'

'Twice,' said Fordham. 'Twice here! We've never had anything like it! Bliss is taking it badly! Hysterical! I've given him a sedative. Look, do you mind if I go now? One or two of the ladies are being a little troublesome too. You won't keep them any longer than you have to?'

'No. Thank you, Doctor.'

When he had gone, Mabbatt growled:

'Not Parsons! He was here! And Bell outside!'

'And Charlie Bliss in the bar,' pointed out Strapp. 'It could always have been accidental, though,' he went on. 'Mrs Bliss, sir.'

Mabbatt was glad to have an object on which to vent his pent-up anger:

'Strapp! Sometimes I think you're short on sense! Sometimes you're downright bloody stupid!'

A knock on the door stopped Strapp's reply. It would not have been conciliatory. But the sergeant choked down his retort when Root gave his message.

'The Assistant Chief's on his way, sir. Here in five minutes.'

The news would have come from of the cars in the neighbourhood. Every policeman in the area would know that the big guns were out.

'Right,' said Mabbatt. 'Everything under control down there?'

'Some tears, sir. A drunk making a nuisance of himself. But a few of the more sober ones are keeping things together.'

Mabbatt had the map of the course out again. The pert little figure of Elaine Bliss had a black ring around it. Strapp watched the Superintendent reinforce the stark blackness of the ring. Then the black-tipped fibre pen hesitated.

It moved to Charlie Bliss, whose head peered out of the bright blue tent with animal-like curiosity. Poor Charlie, thought Strapp. He wouldn't keep his job now. Wife and job gone with one push!

Mabbatt was wondering which of the suspects he would interview first; so much was obvious from his intent stare. Strapp felt dejected. For a few minutes, he had shared Mabbatt's elation when Parsons had so readily admitted his connection with Jenny Piggott. It had not lasted.

Mabbatt looked up, as if remembering him.

'You're not stupid, Sergeant,' he said.

Then he looked down at the map again.

Was this an apology? Sergeant Strapp had not expected one. He did not answer. He remembered Root's doubtful face when he had come in from the Irish match at Mabbatt's insistence. Was Mabbatt floundering? *Had* he missed something? For a few seconds, the pen hovered.

So who was it?

Strapp waited. Then he spoke. He had thought about it first, but he decided to risk Mabbatt's vile temper:

'We can't assume that the two deaths are connected, sir.'

Mabbat looked up.

'What?' he growled.

They both heard the sound of a powerful car arriving. Smooth, gentle, very powerful. The Assistant Chief Constable's unostentatious Daimler.

'It's the maggot farm,' Mabbatt said, in an unusually quiet voice. 'Bloody maggots!' he burst out. 'Maggots!' he bellowed. 'Bloody sodding maggots!'

Strapp could see maggots, millions of them.

Root showed in the Assistant Chief Constable after only a

peremptory knock. As always, he observed a punctilious politeness when speaking to Mabbatt in front of his officers.

'Good evening, Superintendent.'

'Evening, sir.'

Mabbatt was on his feet. The Assistant Chief was not a large man though Strapp considered him the most impressive man he had ever met. He had risen through the ranks, most of the time in the uniformed branches of the force, though it was generally known that he had specialized for some of his service in Security duties.

'I'll see you alone,' the Assistant Chief said.

'Wait outside, Sergeant. And you too, Root.'

They went.

A thought struck Strapp:

'I'd have said he looked like a golfer.'

'He is,' said Root. 'He golfs out in Nottingham,' he told Strapp, mentioning the name of a famous championship course which was notorious for the snobbishness of its members, the vastness of its subscriptions and the impenetrability of its rough. They talked golf for a full ten minutes.

Root needed to think about something other than the broken body of Elaine Bliss. He deliberately shut out the sights he had witnessed. Frank Bell leading Margaret Hughes away, both of them white and shocked, but Frank able to control himself as Margaret screamed thinly until she was led into the quietness of the little lounge used for cosy afternoon teas. Charlie Bliss whimpering and saying it wasn't fair; the steward had started drinking – any glass that came to hand, wine, someone's gin and vermouth, whisky, beer, anything to hold down the rising tide of fear and depression. Ursula, hanging back and asking no questions, but afraid for him, for she had heard of the mad dash by the two policemen to the summit of the tower. Parsons, his jeering laughter changing to dumb revulsion when he saw the body of Elaine Bliss. And a dozen others, who thought that Aspinall had been up to some madness out in the gardens: their anticipatory laughter turning to shocked fear as they saw what a fall of seventy or eighty feet had done to the ripe body of the stewardess.

Cars began to arrive with a crisp authoritativeness.

'Hold on here,' said Strapp.

Root heard the rumble of Mabbatt's voice through the heavy door. What was Mabbatt telling his Chief? That he'd done all that was humanly possible to find the murderer of Tom Tyzack? That he'd attended this, the first gathering of any size since the murder, in order to gain an idea of the personalities of the suspects in the case? That it was too soon to start asking if the two murders were connected? They had to be, thought Root. Poor Elaine Bliss: poor broken Tom Tyzack.

The Assistant Chief Constable had in fact dismissed the latest crime quickly. It wasn't his job to mull over details. Mabbatt outlined the facts. How half-a-dozen people had heard the shriek of the falling woman. The discovery of Lecky's unconscious body. The lack of further information apart from the negative fact that the suspects in the Tyzack case could not have been involved in the second death.

Mabbatt admitted to himself that the Assistant Chief hadn't wasted time in futile questions. No discussion, for instance, of the medical evidence available. He accepted Fordham's assurance that Lecky's wound was no accident; and he did no more than nod when Mabbatt told him that he was treating the case of Elaine Bliss's death as one of murder. But he was interested in Mabbatt's brief report on his latest inquiries into the killing of Tom Tyzack.

'It hinges on the maggot farm?'

'A quarter of a million pounds, sir,' Mabbatt said. He went to thump the desk but thought better of it. 'Money talks. Someone's had access to the Ministry files in London. It has to be, sir!'

'You've seen this place? This *maggot* farm?'

'Yes, sir.'

'I thought you would. Nothing there?'

'The people couldn't be more respectable. Man and wife. No kids. They get a rake-off on turnover. Very efficient. They don't know about the motorway – as they shouldn't! They're happy to think the farm's going to continue. They make plenty.'

'I don't think I'd like to see it.'

'No, sir.'

'So what about the stewardess?'

Mabbatt shrugged.

'You've read about her, sir. She's been the mistress of a number of men at the club. She could have known more than she said. Without realizing it,' he added. 'She wasn't heavy on brains.'

The Assistant Chief nodded.

'A leak in London? Someone passing the route of the motorway for a cut in the profits?'

'There've been cases like that.'

Not in South Yorkshire, but Mabbatt read the papers.

'More my line of country than yours, eh, Mabbatt?'

'I'd say so, sir.'

'Right! I'll get on the phone tonight. Leave the details to me – I'll clear you with someone at the Home Office and get you a telephone number. Whoever it is will liaise with Roads.' The Assistant Chief stood up. 'One more thing, Mabbatt.'

'Sir?'

'Don't try to do it all yourself.'

Mabbatt stood to attention.

'Sir!'

'I want to see an abstract of all statements tomorrow morning, by the way. No details. Just a general picture. Bad business this, Superintendent.'

When he had gone, Mabbatt breathed out slowly. He had been restrained, even self-possessed. The inquiry meant a great deal to him: he coveted a promotion to Chief Superintendent. No, the interview had not gone badly; the Assistant Chief had not suggested that he work any closer with Force Headquarters. He was still in full charge. Professionally he was still in favour. In a year or so, when two or three older men retired, he should move up to Chief Superintendent. He looked down at his massive hands. He began to worry. Two murders instead of one. It smacked of carelessness.

He tore the door open:

'Sergeant!'

'He's with the Assistant Chief Constable, sir,' said Root.

Mabbatt stared at him.

'Sir.'

'What are you doing here?'

Root sighed inwardly. What had the Chief done to Mabbatt? He was glaring like something that should be kept in a cage at night.

'You told me to wait here, sir.'

Mabbatt looked down the stairway where Strapp was talking to a group of senior officers.

'You were a pal of that Lecky?'

'Yes, sir.'

'You should be on bedside duty. Get to the hospital. Don't miss anything! I want a name!'

'Yes, sir.'

It was not an unwelcome duty. As yet Root felt no fatigue at all, in spite of having been up since first light. The booze had worn off too. Waiting beside the unconscious Lecky would be doing something useful. So far, he had contributed nothing that, say, one of the groundsmen couldn't. Local knowledge. No insight into character, no sudden flash of inspiration. PC Plod, he thought. Root felt all of his forty-odd years. PC Plod, fit for village bobbying and frightening teenagers.

Ursula waved to him. He went to her.

'Now what?' she asked.

'I've to stay on duty. I'll be at the hospital out at Firswood.'

'With Jack?'

'Yes.'

Ursula's eyes were full of tears.

'I'll go home with Frank and Margaret. Be careful how you tell him.'

'I will.'

'At least they had the sense to send someone like you, Arthur. You'll know what to say.'

Unaccountably, he felt much better.

Twenty-seven

'In the interest of all, players should play without delay.'

They woke Jack Lecky from three a.m. onwards. He had come out of his dazed, semi-conscious state at about two in the morning.

'Elaine?' he whispered.

The doctor motioned Root to the doorway. He was not a young man. Thin, greying, probably a Bengali by his build. South Yorkshire's hospitals couldn't do without the Empire.

'This Elaine he speaks of?'

'Killed, Doctor. She was the one.'

'Very sad. His wife?'

'No, Doctor. But he was very attached to her.'

'Keep it from him until I tell you.'

'When can he be questioned?'

'This man will not speak for some hours. Get some rest yourself.'

Root knew he wouldn't doze but he said nothing at the curt instruction. One word, that was all he needed. The name of the vicious assailant who had thrown Elaine Bliss from the high tower. The man who had killed Tom Tyzack.

Root accepted a blanket, for the ward was fairly cool. It must be on the north side, thought Root. A thick old building put up by charity money two hundred years ago.

'It'll all be over in the morning,' said Frank Bell on the way home. 'When Jack Lecky wakes up, they'll know who did it. Then it's finished.'

'Yes,' said Margaret, still shaking. 'All finished after tonight.'

For Root the night was a succession of starchy rustles as the nurse shook Lecky until he grunted.

'Morning!' said someone.

It was Strapp.

Root looked at his watch – five to seven.

'Well?' asked Strapp. 'Anything?'

Root passed his notebook.

Strapp read the single line. 'At five a.m. when aroused by a nurse, John Lecky said "No". He was distressed.'

'What about telling him?' Strapp lowered his voice. 'The sooner the better. There's all hell let loose about this. As soon as he wakes if the doctor agrees. Gently, though.'

Five minutes later, Lecky was awake. He saw a nut-brown face behind gold-rimmed spectacles. Then he remembered. In the night there had been the worried eyes and the sharp voices of nurses. The doctor had told him that he had been hurt. An accident?

He tried to sit up.

Memories rushed back, but the pain in his head made him feel sick. He saw Root and the sergeant. Hospital? An accident? His head hurt abominably. Concussed, he told himself. Then: the tower.

Elaine!

He called aloud to the two men.

'Elaine! Arthur – what is it?'

He watched Root's long, tired face. There was no hint of anything in it – it might have been the man who waved you on at the traffic intersections; the man who sold you postage stamps: an impersonal, experienced face. One that had seen this kind of thing before; often. The room swam. Root's face became distant. The Bengali doctor's spectacles shot out streams of light. Lecky shuddered.

'Do you know me?' someone was saying. 'Who am I?'

'The doctor,' began Lecky. 'No.' He opened his eyes. 'The Sergeant.'

'That's right,' said Strapp.

'Yes?' asked Root.

He was talking to the doctor.

'If it's so important, Officer.'

'It is, sir. Two lives – '

Lecky was puzzled by the questions and the abrupt, curtailed answers. Someone was being very, very discreet. And policemen were seldom evasive.

'Right,' said Strapp to Root.

'You were on the roof of the tower, Jack. Do you remember?'

A shape against the pale clouds.

'I was with Elaine.'

He felt afraid. Root should have laughed, made a joke, said *something*. But Root stared at him in that stranger's way.

'It's serious,' Root said. 'You were with Elaine. Who else was there?'

Lecky would have smiled if his head had not hurt so much. Who else should be there? Then he remembered the anxious voices in the night – voices in a car that swayed whilst he lay hurt. Then crisp voices in the night asking him if he was John Lecky. So why so much concern?

'What happened?' he asked.

'An accident,' Root said. 'Serious.'

'The doctor said I wasn't hurt badly. In the night.'

'It's Elaine.'

The black shape hurtling towards him. That hadn't been Elaine. He tried to sit up, but the doctor's hand was on his chest.

'Do not attempt,' said the precise voice. 'Lie back. Bad for your head.'

178

'Where is she? Where!'

He could see it in Root's face now. The official mask slipped and Arthur Root, village bobby and next-door neighbour, was there. He knew that something frightful had happened, something quite different from his own injuries.

'She fell,' Root said. 'I'm sorry, Jack. Elaine's dead. She fell from the tower.'

'Dead? *Dead*!'

'Yes, Jack. What did you see? Was anyone else there? It's very important, Jack.' Root moved closer. The doctor gave way reluctantly. 'Who else was there?'

Lecky groaned. Not twice! Not Elaine gone!

'There was someone, Jack! Who was it?'

'Do not shout,' said the doctor calmly. 'No more questions, please.'

Lecky knew that Arthur Root would go away, and this he could not stand.

'Arthur!'

The doctor raised his hand to stop Root. But Root went on, disregarding him.

'It's important,' he said to doctor and patient. 'Who was there? On the roof.'

'A black shape – just the shape,' Lecky said. 'Not Elaine? She couldn't have been – '

'Did you recognize who it was?'

'No, Arthur. I had a glimpse.'

'A man?'

'Yes.'

'You're sure?'

'Yes.'

'How? How can you be sure? Who was it!'

This time it was Strapp asking the question. But the doctor looked at Lecky's face.

'Definitely no more questions,' he said sharply. 'Please go out. At once!'

Strapp would have refused. He saw, however, that Lecky was

179

deeply distressed. He knew shock when he saw it. That, and concussion; it was a dangerous combination. He went to the door.

'Go home,' he muttered to Root. 'I'll call later. Get a few hours in.' To the doctor, he said: 'Please, Doctor. Over here.'

The Bengali watched Lecky as he lay with tears streaming down his face.

'Well, Sergeant? This man must not be disturbed. Not for some hours.'

'I'll stay, Doctor. But remember, sir, that we're dealing with what we take to be murder. Two murders. My chief will want to know more.'

'You know, Sergeant,' the little Bengali said, 'I am fully conversant with casualty work. This man has told you all he knows. Wait, by all means. But you will not learn any more from him. I am sorry.'

'Thanks, Doctor.'

Root was lucky. He knew one of the car crew which had dropped Strapp off. Root had played cricket against the driver in his pre-golf days. They didn't think it would be straining their operational schedule too much to drop him off at his village. It meant a detour, that was all.

Curly was a bald constable. Root didn't know him well.

'Did he say anything?' Curly asked.

But Root was asleep.

'Leave him be,' said the other. 'He's had his whack.'

Twenty-eight

'A person outside the match may point out the location . . . for which a search is being made.'

On Monday morning, the day after Elaine's death, the national newspapers had woken up to the fact that, whilst the Open was on at Sunningdale and with an English whizz-kid leading two strokes ahead of Nicklaus in the second round, they had a juicy golfing murder on their hands. KILLER ON THE COURSE! GOLF-CLUB GIRL PLUNGES TO DEATH! BOGEY IN CLUBHOUSE! the headlines shrieked. Mabbatt's life had not been easy. Two television men had burst in on him. It wasn't until they were promised a filmed statement that they agreed to go.

That evening, Root was able to watch Mabbatt's large face on Yorkshire Television. He was extremely photogenic, as it turned out. His confident manner, his large prominent nose and ears, his ways of looking into the camera as if it were thinking of making off with his wallet : all made for a splendid interview – so the Producer said – and the establishment of Mabbatt as a television personality.

Over the next day or two, his investigating team interviewed everyone who had been at the Captain's Dance. The huge work of comparing statements had to be done; and, at the same time, the inquiry into Tom Tyzack's death went on at full pressure. And then there was a break.

It started with a phone call, to Mabbatt. After it, he was seen to become almost elated. At midday even the newest recruit to the ranks of the detectives had heard the news: London had come through with something.

'Nothing definite,' the languid voice told Mabbatt. 'But there's been a series of leaks from the Ministry concerning developments — grants, sites, roads. We know which section, but there's no one to point the finger at. Not yet. Give us time.'

Mabbatt stressed the urgency of the inquiry. He got a sigh and an apology.

Yet it was enough to give the hunters fresh impetus, even in the garbled form in which it filtered down to them. The investigation into the deaths of Thomas Geoffrey Tyzack and Elaine Sarah Bliss was seen as purposeful.

Lecky was interviewed twice, both times by Strapp, with Root present. He could talk rationally He had nothing to add to what he had already told the sergeant and Root during his short emergence from unconsciousness on Sunday. The pain was still in his eyes. His hands shook when he spoke of Elaine. Physically, though, he was on the way to recovery.

'You can go home tomorrow,' the Bengali told him as the two policemen were leaving. 'I'll get an ambulance for you. Is there anyone at home to look after you?'

Root answered:

'My wife will, Doctor.'

'All right, Constable. That will be satisfactory.'

The Bengali walked out ahead of them, a straight-backed thin little figure, very sure of himself.

'We'll play golf soon!' Root called to Lecky.

'Thanks for coming,' said Lecky, forgetting that Root was on duty. 'Golf? I don't think I'll be bothering.'

That made Root worry. There was such a vacant look about him that he wondered if his mind was affected by Elaine's death.

'I'll keep an eye on him,' he told the Sister as they left.

'Someone needs to,' she said.

That evening, PC Hunt came to see Root. He was very pleased with himself. He had caught the burglar who had been robbing the local garages.

'You owe me a beer!' he told Root. 'Picked him up as he was coming out of a lock-up garage on the Stone Lane Estate – tools in his pockets, a crowbar in his hand!'

'Who was it?' Root asked.

At least some good had come out of the transfer. One thief caught was one less to worry about.

'Old Cary from the lower village.'

Hunt's burnished face shone with the joy of achievement. Ursula Root banged a pair of glasses down for them. She'd be piqued, thought Root. It was his patch, his village.

'Have a beer then, lad,' he said. 'Now tell me about it.'

They settled down in comfort. Hunt began his account of the capture of old Cary. It was a pleasant part of police life, hearing the mass of detail in a successful arrest. It took an hour, and then Hunt asked:

'Now what about the investigation up at the golf club?'

Root was glad of the opportunity for a talk. Hunt was a likeable young man. He had enthusiasm and patience, so much was certain. And he hadn't made the mistake of trying to clear up the whole of the village's crime in one week. One thing especially pleased Root: he'd left the Smethurst boy alone. The lad had been behaving himself, so Hunt had let the drug business fade away. It wasn't good law perhaps, but it was good village bobbying.

'It could be they've got something, but I don't see that it's going to catch Tom Tyzack's murderer. No! We've missed something – something about one of those people in the spinney. There's someone who couldn't bear to have Tom alive. And Elaine Bliss! You know,

I'm old-fashioned in a lot of ways – oh, I am!' he insisted, as Hunt began to interrupt. 'I talk a lot to people. I see kids and I stop to tell them to tie up their laces or take their little sister home. And I do my garden with compost – old-fashioned, you see. And I'm old-fashioned about murder, lad. Murder's not something like stealing tools or bricks.' He was distracted for a moment. 'Have you any ideas about the bricks yet? No? Well, it'll keep.' Then he went on: 'Murder's not just violence – you've got to use either a lot of skill or a lot of force to kill someone. I've seen people so badly knocked about you'd swear they couldn't live – blood everywhere. And they've been on their feet two weeks later. There just hasn't been the determination to kill. A killer's got to have it – he's got to want someone dead. Dead. Stone dead. And that's what I think's wrong up at Wolvers. We're not getting to the determination to kill.'

Hunt nodded.

'The psychology of the murderer, eh? I did a paper on that in training. Got a bad grade, though. It was out of fashion three years back. I expect it'll be in again now.'

'It isn't psychology,' said Root. 'It's people. I reckon Tom must have done something that grew and grew in someone's mind until he couldn't see Tom walking about with that smile he mostly had.'

As he said it, Root felt again the inadequacy of his words. PC Plod talking again of matters beyond him!

'So you've no favourites?'

Hunt knew of course that Margaret Hughes' young man had come under suspicion. And he had read the newspaper innuendoes that suggested in a delicate way that Charlie Bliss might have had a hand in at least one of the murders. Hunt looked at Root keenly. He wished that he could change places with him.

'Favourites?' Root said. He finished his beer. 'They've all been scratched at the post. And the outsiders aren't showing at all. I've always felt this is one that's going to take time.'

'Don't be too long about it,' said Hunt, not altogether in a kindly way. 'This village isn't exactly my cup of tea.'

He took his leave, not fogetting to thank Ursula for her hospitality. When he had gone, Root realized what a strain the past ten days had been. Ursula saw that he was sleepy.

'I'll lock up,' she said. 'You go on.'

Root nodded. He hoped that Mabbatt would not find a reason for calling him out. And he reminded himself to check on the procedure for payment of his expenses. He hadn't been reimbursed yet for the drinks and petrol he had put in a claim for.

When he got to bed he couldn't sleep right away.

They had missed something. That was what he had said to Hunt. Tom Tyzack's death had been *intentional*. But why? *Why!* It made no sense when you knew that Jenny Piggott got the maggot farm.

No sense at all!

Before he did sleep, however, Root remembered what he had said to Hunt; that they had missed something at the course. He was sure of it. The last thing he thought of as he turned to Ursula was the shadowy figure of a ball-scavenger merging with the dappled greenery.

Twenty-nine

'The player is the sole judge . . .'

Information accumulated. Mabbatt sent a Chief Inspector to London. He returned the same day with more unclear evidence. It was easy enough, the fairly high-ranking security official possessed of the languid voice admitted, easy enough if you knew the ropes. You could get through to almost any Ministry department, and, if you had the confidence, the right accent, and a working knowledge of the procedures of the place, you could find out almost anything you wanted. All you did was to say that you were a member of another Ministry department, that you needed the information in a hurry because someone was breathing down your neck, and, as likely as not, you'd get what you wanted.

So far there was no one to point the finger at, but there were certain directions in which one might cast a glance. Ex-employees, for instance. Just suppose one managed to get financial backing . . .

'It's not specific, sir', said the Chief Inspector. 'But it's a start.

What shall we do?'

'Hope!' Mabbatt grunted. 'Hope we find the bloody golf-stick! Hope the villain cracks! Hope your lot turn something up! And keep looking!'

Mabbatt turned again to the map of the course showing the spinney. Elaine Bliss's neat caricature smiled fixedly at him. Even now, Mabbatt could not look at her pert figure without scowling; but it attracted him nevertheless. He looked at it closely for a full minute.

Then, impulsive animal that he was, he rang Jenny Piggott.

'I'd like to come to see you again, Miss Piggott.'

'Oh?'

Jenny Piggott's voice was hostile.

'I need to have a word,' said Mabbatt.

He kept his eyes on the tiny, smiling figure.

'What for?'

Mabbatt couldn't have answered honestly, for he didn't know. Premonition? Impulse? He shook his ponderous head.

'It'll be tonight,' he said.

'Tonight!'

'I'll call in on my way home.'

'I'm going out!'

Mabbatt couldn't think of an answer. He was possessed by a comparatively calm feeling of need. Jenny Piggott sensed it.

'Are you there?'

'Yes,' said Mabbatt.

'I'll be in after ten.'

The mutual hostility seemed to drain away as the telephone conversation ended. Mabbatt got to his feet and went out to look at the searchers. The Army had sent their two top men with even more remarkable devices. And the bulldozer had scooped out the pond that ran alongside the second fairway. In the mud they found two thousand, three hundred and nineteen golf-balls. No murder weapon was recovered.

'On your own?' Jenny Piggott said.

'Aye.'

'Where's your sergeant?'

'Gone home, if he's any sense.'

'Come in. I've just got back from bingo. Out at Malton. I didn't win anything.'

She felt excitement and extreme discomfort. It was a strange sensation. Mabbatt's bulk and his ponderous movements brought her almost to panic. She clung to the notion that, however aggressive and bloody-minded he was, he represented authority. He was a policeman.

Mabbatt stood watching her as earlier he had stared at the tiny figure of Elaine Bliss.

'Were it about Tom?' asked the woman.

Her wide-set eyes were a vivid sea-green; Mabbatt didn't see them. He was staring at the white flesh of her bosom. She put a hand to her throat.

'Were there something about Tom?'

Now she was trembling.

Mabbatt sat down, without invitation.

'There is,' he told her.

Her voice was hoarse.

'What?'

'Someone put him on to that maggot farm.'

Jenny smoothed her dress.

'I went to see it. It stinks.'

'Thomas Tyzack bought it for a reason.'

'I know. Mr Robinson told me. They're going to build a motorway café there.'

'Someone told him to buy the farm.'

'Well I don't know who it were!'

'Don't you?'

The woman felt faint. Mabbatt's great bulk took up most of the settee. His legs blocked her off from the doorway.

'No,' she whispered.

'Was it Robinson?'

The woman swallowed nervously.

'I don't know – I don't want the farm! T'bungalow's enough – and

I've got money.' She waved to the drinks cabinet. 'I can work. Do you want a drink?'

Mabbatt nodded.

'Aye. Whisky.'

'I'll get you one!'

Mabbatt got to his feet.

Jenny Piggott found herself facing him.

Gruffly, and with an attempt at an apology, he said:

'I didn't think you knew anything.'

She turned away.

'I'll get your drink.'

'Just a minute.'

'What?'

Mabbatt licked his lips.

'That day I came.'

'Which?'

'The last time you'd got the booze out.'

'Well?'

'Someone was coming.'

Jenny Piggott tried to smile; she looked scared.

'It were only the woman from next door.'

'Were it.'

'Yes.'

She went towards him and Mabbatt reached for her.

'I'm here on official business.'

'Are you,' she said, turning her face up to him.

'Aye!'

News of Mabbatt's romantic involvement with an important witness was rumoured through the investigating team by Friday. Nothing was said. He was becoming a celebrity. A local newspaper ran a feature on THE BIG MAN WITH THE REPUTATION FOR SUCCESS. Yorkshire television showed the interview they had wrung from him once more, with a two-minute commentary on his forthright views. Mabbatt was a natural.

On Friday, Strapp talked to Root at the end of a week's gruelling work. They had finished a day of cross-checking statements. Strapp had wanted to ask Root's opinion of the way the investigation was going. At first the older man was reluctant to air his views. For one thing, Strapp was a sergeant. For another, Strapp was a Mabbatt man. However, Strapp kept at it until Root began, very circumspectly, to put forward his opinions.

'You don't say much,' said Strapp. 'Cagey?'

'I'm a village bobby,' Root said. 'You lads are the detective team. I'll tell you all I know, but I don't run to doing your job.'

'You can't have long to do?'

'Two years for the pension.'

'It wouldn't harm to say what you think.'

'No?'

'Not with two years to go. It's past six. We can be spared. Come and have a beer.'

'Aye,' said Root. 'It's been a long day.'

Charlie Bliss assumed an expression of deep mourning when they appeared. Half-a-dozen people were in the bar. Fordham was with Philip Church. Bliss pulled two pints of beer. Root half-listened to Fordham's talk of the invention that would enable a golfer to read the contours of the greens – and still be acceptable to the Royal and Ancient.

Strapp waited until Bliss had gone.

'You're not saying then?' he asked.

'I've had my own ideas,' Root told him.

'I'd like to hear them.'

So Root told him what he had said to PC Hunt.

'I've been detecting in a small way for twenty years,' he said. 'I'm trying to catch a bloke at the moment. He steals bricks – not many at a time. He gets them away night after night. I don't know how he does it. But I'll catch him, because I can wait. The trouble is, I can't see why he wants them. I've tried doing the usual things – asking who's building an outhouse, who's doing a bit of work at the weekend. Who wants a rustic brick wall or something like that – but I can't get anywhere near it. But I will, because I know the people all round. I reckon I'll catch him when I hear a whisper from someone I know. By chance. It's all to do with people. How people think. What people notice.'

He paused to drink from his pint pot.

'Mabbatt's missing out on psychology?'

'You've been to college too?'

Strapp grinned.

'Don't try the thick village-bobby stuff with me. I reckon you could have made Sergeant fifteen years ago if you'd wanted.'

Root had begun to like Strapp.

'I wasn't bothered about promotion.'

'Go on about Mabbatt.'

Root found it difficult. He considered his beer for some time. Fordham's thin, reedy voice piped away about posture and alignment of bones. Bones, plumb-lines and contours. Root half-listened, for it sounded as though Fordham might have something.

At last, Root summed up what had been worrying him for the past week. He pushed putting and plumb-lines out of his mind.

'I reckon there's too much paper getting in the way,' he said.

'Paper?'

This did puzzle Strapp.

'Aye, paper. You remember last week when we walked over the course checking angles and positions?'

'From the statements. Yes.'

'Then when Bliss and the others were questioned – it was all statements.'

'That's the way it's done.'

'But it's all paper!' Root said. He surprised himself by his vehemence. 'There's so much bloody paper, we can't see what's really happened. We're taking all those statements and numbers and angles as gospel. Suppose they're not? I mean, suppose things aren't what they're written down as?'

Strapp finished off his beer too.

'Too much taken for granted?' he asked. 'Is that what you think?'

'Maybe. But we'll get this one sorted out the way I'll find my brick-thief – a whisper from someone. Someone remembering something.

People's minds going click-click and then you've got him.'

'So what would you do?'

'I'd talk to the people who see everything – the ground-staff, the bar-staff, the scroungers – I'd just *talk* to them. And let them talk.'

'The scroungers?' said Strapp.

He was interested.

'Especially Williamson.'

'Why don't you?'

'He hasn't been seen here since the murder.'

'Find him!'

'I'm not CID.'

Strapp grinned.

'You want to, don't you?'

'Yes!'

'Then do it!'

'I will,' said Root, surprised at his own confidence. 'I will.'

Strapp leaned over the bar to press the bell for Bliss. The steward was not in sight.

Just as he reached upwards, however, he said:

'Good God!'

Root turned to see what had caused his exclamation.

'Jack!' he said in astonishment. 'What are you doing here!'

Everyone watched as Jack Lecky walked up to Root.

Thirty

'A "rub of the green" occurs when a ball . . . is stopped or deflected by an outside agency.'

Jack Lecky looked haggard. The back of his head was still taped. Root noticed Fordham's professional gaze. He moved forward.

'Jack! You should be at home – isn't Ursula looking after you?'

'I'm all right, Arthur, thanks. I couldn't stay in the house any longer. I've been sitting around for three days and I get sick of it. No, I'm all right,' he insisted. 'The doctor at the hospital said I should try a little exercise when I felt better. I thought I'd have a walk. Can't sit and mope endlessly.'

Bliss came through the partition at the back of the bar. He saw Lecky. For a moment, Root thought there might be trouble. But Bliss had decided to be noble.

'Can I get you anything, sir?' he asked Lecky solicitously. 'Drop of brandy if you're not feeling too good?'

Lecky was hideously embarrassed.

'Yes, yes,' he muttered. 'Brandy.'

'Good to see you on your feet, Mr Lecky.'

Bliss bowed in a small, polite gesture.

Lecky looked at Root. He seemed to be making up his mind. Then he said.

'I'm very sorry about Mrs Bliss.'

Bliss allowed a hint of his customary malice to show in his eyes.

'Thank you, sir. She'll be sadly missed all round.'

'Come and sit down, Jack,' said Root. He included Strapp in the invitation. 'How did you come? Car?'

'Bus.'

'Then come back with me. I'm off in a few minutes.'

'I thought I'd have a walk. A look at the course.'

Root felt some relief. It was the first time Lecky had shown any interest in golf since the brutal attack on Saturday night.

Strapp put in:

'I don't think so, Mr Lecky. You don't look up to it yet. Go back with Arthur.'

There was a bustle of noise around Fordham's table.

'Here's Frank!' called Church. 'We'd better go and change.'

Fordham got to his feet. He walked over to the table where Root and the others were sitting.

'Hello,' he said to Lecky. 'Feeling better now? Got over the knock?'

'Just about, thanks.'

Fordham looked closely at him.

'Don't rush things, young man,' he said. 'You've plenty of time for golf. Wolvers will still be here in a fortnight's time.'

'He's going back home with me,' said Root.

'Right, Arthur. We're knocking round with young Bell and Des Purseglove. Frank's here. Des comes ready changed.' He patted Lecky on the shoulder. 'We'll have a game when you're fit. I see your membership's through. Glad to have you.'

Just then, Purseglove's oldish Vauxhall swung into view.

'Here's Des – we'll take his money tonight! Well, good-bye!'

'Look at old Fordham. Over seventy,' said Root in admiration.

'And still winning competitions. He's got the best run-up shots I've ever seen. For a club golfer, that is. He once played with Vardon.'

Strapp hadn't heard of Vardon, so they talked golfing history for the better part of an hour. Lecky looked better by this time, but Root was determined to see him home. There was a sense of pure grief about Lecky that disturbed him deeply; he wasn't going to recover quickly, however soon his head wound healed. Golf was the answer, he thought: on the golf course nothing got in the way. You were in such a torment about the lie of your ball, the state of the greens, the strength of the wind, the anxiety of being one down with three to play, and the unbearable tension of seeing your partner's ball fly out of bounds so that you *had* to get your tee-shot off well, that you forgot business worries and dead mistresses. Lecky got on to the golden days of golf. And, gradually, his voice lost some of its overtones of melancholy.

At seven, Root said:

'Come on. Time we went. Nothing else, is there, Sergeant?'

Strapp grinned:

'Come back with our man.'

Root was struck by a sudden longing to be off the case. He asked Strapp if there was any prospect of being sent back to his normal duties.

Strapp grinned again. 'No chance. Back here tomorrow at eight-thirty, Constable Root. One of the Inspectors wants to do some pacing out of distances. He knows all about statistics. You'll be on hand to help him. I'm here for another hour going over his plans.'

'Good night, sir,' said Bliss gravely to Lecky.

Lecky remembered what Elaine had said about her husband. A nowt man. A nothing man. The rat-faced steward began polishing a glass. Lecky felt an urge to shout across to the blank, bland steward that he should be man enough to show some sign of remorse or sorrow. His head began to ache.

Parsons stopped the two men:

'Hello, Arthur! You all right now?' he said to Lecky. 'You were lucky, weren't you? Nearly lost a new member – bad for trade, that. What about that bastard Mabbatt?' he asked Root. 'He's fixed up with Jenny Piggott! I wouldn't trust any of your lot with a dying grandmother!' To Lecky he added: 'They're the biggest whoremasters, these coppers. I'll see you around, eh, Jack?'

Root recognized Lecky's pain and anger at Parsons' crassness.

'Leave it, Jack,' he said. 'He's going soon.'

Lecky saw the path where Elaine had died. There were stains on the old, worn stone. Anger again flooded through him. Why kill a woman like Elaine? What could a woman like her have done to deserve such a death! Why *Elaine*!

Root saw the strained expression and began to worry. He had seen it before. Violence was not far away.

'Come on, Jack,' he said. 'Let's get back. Ursula will have some supper for us.'

Lecky looked back at the residual traces on the stone.

'Why her!'

'That'll do!' Root said. 'We'll see to it.'

'Will you?'

Root's worries redoubled. Again he doubted Mabbatt and his methods. And again he told himself that a village bobby was not in a position to criticize a Superintendent. Especially when the Superintendent was a man called Mabbatt, with a successful record. Lecky's doubts reinforced his own. But he could say nothing for Lecky's comfort. He said sharply:

'It's not your concern! You've got to get yourself back to a fit state for golf, Jack. The past's past! Now, no more of this – get in the car.'

He turned the old Hillman into the wide, tree-lined drive. As always he had time to spare a glance at the first fairway and the tiny patterned green beyond.

Then, in the bushes, a few yards from the car, he saw Williamson. His decision was immediate.

'Hold on here, Jack. Will you? I'd like a word with him.'

He pointed to the dark-suited figure, but Williamson had completely merged into the background.

'Will you be all right, Jack?'

'Yes, Arthur.'

Root hesitated, but his policeman's soul took him in charge.

'Come out!' he called. 'Sam!'

'Me, Mr Root?'

'Yes! I won't keep you!'

Williamson emerged from the bushes.

'We haven't seen you for a while,' said Root easily. 'Been busy, Sam?'

'They wouldn't let me on t'course!'

Williamson was aggrieved. He had temporarily lost his beer-money.

'But you're back,' said Root. 'Found many?'

'A few.' Williamson patted his pockets. 'Not many. Your lot's taken them all.'

'Now, Sam,' said Root. Something was tugging at his mind. He couldn't find the right words, but the image was there: the one he had gone to sleep thinking about the other night.

'Aye?'

'Funny business,' he offered. 'The other day. You know, Tom getting his head knocked in.'

'I've seen men like that in the pit.'

'How's the arms?'

'Not too bad.'

Root looked back at Lecky. He had his head in his hands. He was wasting his time with Williamson.

'And it's not worth your while coming, is it, Sam?' he asked, thinking of his own failure.

'Too many at it, Mr Root.'

'That so?'

Root turned to go.

'Even daft buggers from t'daft school.'

Root pulled a tenpenny piece from his pocket. Williamson knew the score. He had been interrogated, and he would expect a reward.

'Daft buggers?' he said, his mind only half on Williamson's mumbled comment.

'Aye! They shouldn't be out! Shouldn't be let out!'

Root remembered a vacant face in the shrubbery; and a merging of shadows. And of Parsons complaining that a 'daft lad' had been turned off the course.

'What was that, Sam?'

'Nowt!'

'Have a pint with me,' said Root.

It had been a waste of time after all.

'Nice of you, Mr Root. What's wrong with your mate?'

Lecky was sobbing. Root walked quickly to the car. He waved to Williamson and tried to calm down Jack Lecky.

'Why Elaine! Why *her*! It isn't human, Arthur – at least Tyzack could have had enemies, but Elaine! She never harmed anyone! She couldn't!'

Root wondered whether he should call Fordham from the course. It looked as though Jack Lecky might need a sedative.

'Calm down, Jack,' he ordered 'There's no use getting yourself worked up. I know how you feel. It was one of the worst things I had to do, telling you about it in the hospital. I know how things were working out between you and Elaine.' He watched Lecky's white face. 'Best quieten down, Jack. We'll find you somewhere to sleep at home tonight.'

'She was killed, Arthur! Killed – deliberately!'

Lecky spoke as if somehow Root were doubting him.

'She's dead, Jack, and no amount of shouting can help!'

Lecky shook his head. He gradually recovered.

'No. There's no helping it.'

'You all right?'

'Yes, Arthur.'

Root started the car again.

The Hillman grunted into life and rattled along the uneven road between the two sections of the course south of Wolvers Hall. Root had the driver's window down to catch the wind. He glanced at Lecky. Get him home, Root decided. Try food and tea and then think again about medical assistance.

They passed the thirteenth tee and saw Fordham and Church down the fairway; Frank Bell and Des Purseglove were with them. Frank was shooting for the thirteenth green.

Automatically Root slowed to a crawl. It was part of the etiquette at Wolvers. You didn't disturb a player. They must have decided to play the back six holes first, thought Root, perhaps because the first had been busy. So they teed off a few minutes before on the thirteenth.

The fairway was beside the road. When someone was taking a shot, you didn't disturb their concentration. Frank's drive had outdistanced the others'. He'd been playing a nine or an eight-iron to the green.

Church waved in acknowledgement of Root's courtesy. Purseglove wagged a club too. But Fordham stared hard at Jack Lecky.

Root realized that Jack Lecky was not watching Frank Bell's shot. He was gazing ahead still, quite entranced by his own despair. Bad, thought Root. Bad!

Frank hit another beauty.

High and straight the ball curved into the heavy air, a white streak against the sombre clouds. It exploded. It exploded into the green, bit, and bounced back towards the pin.

If it had been Trevino or Nicklaus, thought Root, the gallery would have gone mad. They'd have roared their appreciation and assured one another that the ordinary club golfer couldn't make that kind of shot. And here was Frank Bell, not an especially good golfer, throwing one up like a champion! Root smiled, his mind wholly on golf. Perhaps Frank's handicap would come down to what it should be – single figures – now that he'd got that Tyzack business off his mind.

'Why?' whispered Lecky quietly.

Root realized that he could move off. It would be as well to get Jack home quickly; it had done him no good at all, this visit to Wolvers. He put the worn gears into play and the Hillman slid forward. They moved past Purseglove and Church. One of them had sliced off into the sycamores, to the right of the thirteenth; both went to look for it. There were two balls on the green – Frank's, of course, two feet or so from the pin; and another, on the far side of the green. Purseglove's, Root decided, for Fordham was walking towards a ball fifty yards short of the green. All this passed through his analytical golfer's mind in the time it took him to drive from the point where

Frank had played, to the green itself.

'We'll soon be home, Jack!' he said. 'And we'll have you fit for golf again. A couple of weeks, as Fordham says. Eh, Jack?'

'Golf?' said Lecky.

'Yes, man!'

Root knew the cure for Jack's malaise. Time and the glorious uncertainties of golf would do wonders for him.

'I'll tell you what we'll do, Jack,' he began. He registered the quick, shuffling gait of the small man who ran from the sycamores and on to the green. 'What's he — ' he said, the Hillman clattering across a section of rutted, pot-holed ground.

Lecky was still in his private world of grief.

'I thought he was on the fair — ' Root said aloud, very puzzled. They were at the main road. He halted, careful because the tankers and articulated lorries from Sheffield tore along this stretch of road at sixty. 'Jack, who was that on the green?' he asked as he engaged first gear.

'Who?'

'Yes, Jack!'

A gap appeared in the traffic. Root ignored it. He moved the car to the side of the drive. Odd glimpses and memories began to take shape in his mind; he examined them with something like amazement building up inside him: and then excitement.

Lecky was not much help, but he had to ask someone.

'Jack! On the green — the thirteenth! Didn't you see a little fellow — he ran on, he did, Jack!'

Jack Lecky recognized the urgency in Arthur Root's tones. 'Yes. Out of the woods. In a red jacket. He picked a ball up — '

'In a red jacket!' Root whispered. 'What was he doing? I looked away — I was watching the road — Jack, who was it?'

'I don't know.' Lecky too grasped at memories. 'He was picking a ball up — taking it. He ran off. Back into the trees.'

'A ball-scavenger!'

'Arthur, what — '

Root exploded with one short curse. Now, the memories had merged and formed themselves into an incredible pattern. He thought of Williamson's useless information, and then of the way the scrounger could slide into the background and become a part of the course itself. He remembered a stupid, blank face peering from the trees not far from where he was now sitting in the Hillman. Only one thing was needed for the pattern to become a coherent whole.

'Jack, what did he look like!'

'Who?'

'The fellow on the green! The thirteenth – just now!'

'I don't know.'

'His face!'

'What?'

Root didn't want to put the words into Lecky's mouth. Lecky had to tell him independently what he had seen.

Root thought of the tiny white spot a few inches from the border of the incredibly green carpet, and the way a smallish hand grabbed eagerly; he had retained the impression without quite realizing what was happening. Lecky was confused and in pain, but he had to *think*!

'What did he look like!' Root said urgently.

Lecky concentrated. Something like horror began to fill his eyes.

'His face – a nutter! But when he turned to go into the trees –'

'Yes!'

'Arthur, it couldn't be – not him! It fits – the Irish match! But he couldn't, not Elaine, not when she'd been –'

His words were lost as Root savagely reversed the old Hillman. There was no doubt left in Root's mind. Lecky's identification, confused and incoherent as it was, had convinced him. He had been ready to remain impartial until then, a member of the constabulary who listened to all that was said and then – and not before – made up his mind. But now he was committed to a wild guess. All his previous inhibitions about interfering in the course of the investigations into Tom Tyzack's killing and Elaine Bliss' brutal murder slipped away: he had the scent of the quarry.

'It has to be,' whispered Lecky, appalled. 'When the kid turned, it was *him*!'

Root turned the car and drove fast for the thirteenth green.

Thirty-one

'A "water hazard" is any sea, lake, pond, river, ditch ... or other open water course ...'

Fordham was examining his putt. Frank Bell was nowhere in sight, nor was Purseglove. Church stepped out of the sycamores just as Root brought the Hillman to a violent halt.

'Hello, Arthur,' called Fordham. He saw Lecky's strained face: 'You should be at home!'

'Where are the others?' snapped Root.

Fordham was examining a repaired pitch-mark which lay on his line.

He looked up:

'Des? Frank?'

'Where are they!'

Fordham chuckled. 'Don't ask me! Why?'

He noticed the urgency and authority in Root's voice.

'Where are they?' he repeated. 'Why – '

'Off after that lad!' yelled Church. 'Never seen such a thing in all my years at the club! Stepped onto the green, calm as you please, lifted Des's ball and was off like a shot rabbit! Arthur – you're a policeman: get after him!'

'Which way!'

'There!'

He pointed to the thick woods to the north of the course.

'What's going on, Arthur?' asked Fordham, who sensed that there was more to the situation than a case of stealing, however audacious.

Root hesitated for a moment.

'Dr Fordham. I want you to get to the clubhouse at once. Find a police officer. Sergeant Strapp, if he's there. Tell him that I'm going after a possible suspect in the Tyzack case. And make it quick – can you drive my car?'

'Had a Hillman once.'

'What?' burbled Church. 'What, Root! You don't mean – You can't!'

'I'm coming,' said Lecky.

Lecky was near to collapsing.

'No! Get a message to Superintendent Mabbatt. Explain it to him! You'll do more good that way Jack!'

'Get him, Arthur!'

Root was already running for the wood.

'What shall I do?' asked Church.

Lecky's head felt as if it was bursting.

'Can you tell me about it?' asked Fordham.

Lecky looked back to see Root running hard into the black wood.

'He killed Elaine,' Lecky said, almost unbelievingly. 'Murdered her! Threw her off the tower – how could he!'

Fordham drove faster. Lecky needed sedating. It was going to be a difficult half-hour.

Strapp was still in the Secretary's office. He was looking through an expert analysis of times and distances. Although he had not been convinced by Root's argument about excessive paperwork, he thought he might have a point.

Lecky burst into the room, almost babbling.

'Good God!' exclaimed Strapp. 'You should be home!'

Fordham followed a second or two later. He breathed heavily, and for a moment he couldn't speak. Strapp thought Lecky had gone out of his mind and that Dr Fordham was trying to restrain him. Strapp moved easily towards the distraught figure.

'Don't worry!' he said heartily. 'What's the trouble, Mr Lecky?'

'Listen!' Fordham said, recovering his breath. 'Listen, Sergeant. This is vital!'

Strapp was dialling before Lecky and Fordham were through. So the village bobby was right after all! He felt distinctly pleased at the thought. Yet his expression was serious. A vicious murderer was on the loose. There could be no slip-up in the handling of the matter.

'Who is it?' growled Mabbatt.

Strapp explained in half-a-dozen sentences. At one stage, when he told Mabbatt that Root himself had set off in pursuit of the suspect, he blasted a question down the phone; he made no comment during the remainder of the short message.

'Stay there,' Mabbatt ordered.

The machinery of the Force began to glide into action. Strapp looked a question.

'I'll get him a sedative soon,' said the doctor. 'He's done enough today.'

'I should have gone after him,' Lecky muttered.

'Oh, no!' Fordham said. 'Leave it to Arthur. Take my word for it, young man, Arthur Root's got it well in hand.'

Root crashed through brambles in full flower, over dead logs from the big storms of the whirlwind year, past the occasional rhododendron bush; Root tried to listen as he plunged on noisily, but he heard only the sound of his own passage and the traffic and a dog barking in one of the houses near the course. He stopped. Had he done the right thing? Might it not have been better to get a message personally to Strapp or Mabbatt? And was there really much danger of another brutal killing?

He reached the high wall that marked the boundary of Wolvers Hall. It was easy to scale. Root looked up and down the road. Frank Bell was just about to climb back over the wall.

'Frank!' yelled Root urgently. 'Where are they?'

Frank Bell was chuckling quietly.

'You've never seen such a pantomime!' he called. 'A lad pinched Des's ball, and Des went mad – he's gone after him!' Root jumped down and ran to him. 'Why, Arthur,' said Frank. He saw the grim expression on Root's face. 'What's the trouble?'

'Where is he!'

Frank's face registered shock.

'Des?'

'Where!'

'Purseglove?'

Root nodded impatiently.

'The lad jumped on a bus – Des went after him.'

'Where?'

'He ran for the bus and got it.'

'Which way?'

Frank pointed: 'The Barnsley bus.'

Root rapped out a series of instructions.

'Get to the clubhouse. Tell the police I'm going after him – watch out for police cars. They'll be coming soon. Tell the first policeman you see where I am. Got it?'

Root stepped off the road into the path of an oncoming Ford. The driver shook his fist and swerved to avoid him.

'Stop!' bawled Root, but the car was gone in a swirl of acceleration.

A bread van roared past, and again Root stepped out dangerously close. He waved his hands furiously. The young man at the wheel waved back and put his foot firmly down on the brake. Traffic hurtled past as Root ran to the passenger side.

'Out!' he yelled to the young man's assistant.

'You what!'

'Police – a dangerous criminal!' snapped Root. 'Out – and get

205

moving!'

'You *what*?' the assistant gasped, a local youth by the sound of him. 'You – '

'Get out, Sammy!' his driver said. 'Police – get out, kid!'

'You what!'

But Root was hauling at him. The dazed boy watched the bread-van roar off down the road.

'You're the police?' the driver asked.

'Yes! Can't you go faster?'

The young man laughed.

'Aye.'

The van surged forward.

'Who is it?' the young driver wanted to know. 'Hold-up?'

He shot past the Ford whose driver would not stop for Root. The driver looked up; his mouth fell open and he shook a fist at them.

Root began to answer that he was after a man who could help with an inquiry, but he stopped. Supposing, after all, he had put together two events that were completely unrelated? As they thundered under a railway bridge, Root could visualize himself in front of Mabbatt, stammering out the unlikely tale. About how a man could be seen and not seen at the same time; about the extraordinary coincidence that had given the killer an alibi that had stood up under the close scrutiny of experts. And that a chance remark had shown the killer how his alibi might be shattered!

The bread-van braked suddenly.

'Traffic lights,' said the driver. 'Road repairs.' He glanced at Root. 'You are police, aren't you? I mean, you're not having me on?'

'Yes! And get moving – keep sounding your horn – turn your headlights on, and *get moving*!'

'Right you are! I've always fancied doing this!'

The driver was young enough to enjoy the experience. He waved back at the furious drivers of coaches, lorries and cars. The bread-van's horn blared out, its lights blazed on, and they were out on the open road within half-a-minute.

'Is it thieves?' the driver said again. 'Hold-up?'

Root realized that he had not answered the question.

206

His self-doubts gone, he said:

'A killer.'

'Jesus!'

Then, beyond a bend that followed the curve of a derelict canal cutting, Root saw the familiar red bus.

At the same time, the driver groaned.

'The bloody cakes!'

'Get past that bus and pull in front of it!'

'Right! But my bloody cakes are all over the road – the doors came open at the lights!'

Root stuck his head out of the window and looked back. Trays of cakes bounced backwards, cream-cones, sugar fancies, doughnuts, apple tarts, éclairs, chocolate macaroons, trifles, and marzipans – and with them a shower of slices of bread as far as the eye could see.

If matters hadn't stood so desperately, thought Root, I could laugh my bloody socks off. Instead, he said:

'Stop the bus and wait, will you?'

'Right! I hope they'll pay for my cakes and bread. Will they?'

'I'll ask,' Root promised.

The van eased the bus into the side. Passengers crowded to the front of the bus to demand an explanation and witness the forthcoming encounter. The driver leapt from his cab and met Root with a splutter of rage:

'Who d'you think you are, you silly sod!'

'Police!'

The conductor came running too.

'What's it about, Bill?'

The bread-van driver answered:

'Murder!'

Root jumped into the bus.

'A lad of about fourteen!' he shouted. 'Anyone seen him? Wearing a red anorak!'

'A lad?' the conductor said. 'With an anorak?'

A middle-aged woman with a tiny long-haired dog answered:

'He got off last stop. Again the canal.'

Root caught something from her tone.

'Do you know him?'

'I've seen him before. He's called Willie. Willie Briggs. Goes to special school for dafties. Comes from t'ouses along by canal. Why, what's he done?'

'Did anyone else get off?'

The conductor thought for a second or two.

'Aye. A feller.'

'What did he look like?'

'Not big,' said the conductor.

'He were hot,' said the middle-aged woman. 'Sweaty.'

Root ran.

'Did you say lad's a murderer? I wouldn't believe it,' the woman called. But she was talking only to the open-mouthed conductor by this time, for Root was in the van again and urging the driver to make his best speed.

They reached the canal as the first police car came howling up the road, lights on and siren sounding.

Root reached for the horn; there was an answering howl.

'Stay here!' Root yelled to the driver.

He crashed through the bushes between the disused canal and the road; beyond was a towpath leading to a shabby terrace. This had to be where the boy lived.

He ran.

Behind him, he heard the thudding of boots.

He was the first to see the body.

He lay face down in the canal. There was an uncanny resemblance to the killer. Root dived cleanly in a racing dive that kept him on the surface. It was almost a ridiculous anti-climax to find that he could stand in the canal with his shoulders above the level of the greasy, black water.

'Pass him out!' yelled the first of the car men.

Root was glad to hear a familiar voice. It was the crew who had given him a lift home the Sunday before. The cricketer and his mate, Curly. He pushed the boy over. There was no sign of life – the mouth was open and the eyes looked blankly and stupidly up at the sky with no hint of a reaction to light. Root struggled through the sticky mud.

He pushed against sharp metal, grazing his thigh against some nameless piece of rubbish. The boy floated, so it was easy to get him to the side.

The cricketing policeman left it to his bald mate to apply the kiss of life.

'Did you see him?'

'No,' said Root. 'But we've got him now.'

'Half the force is on the way, Arthur. Hope they don't skid on the cakes. We did.' He looked with a professional eye at the white, mongoloid face.

'Good lad, Curly,' he told his mate. 'You've done it.'

Curly breathed into the slack, cold mouth.

'You have a go,' he said, after a moment. 'I'm puffed.'

The cricketer breathed life deeply into the boy.

There was a trembling about the eyelids.

Mabbatt came as the boy began to giggle in a strange, lunatic delirium. Only then did a slovenly woman come out of one of the terraced houses. She looked about the company of large, serious-faced policemen.

' 'E's fallen in agen, then,' she said. 'I told him not to play by canal.'

Root felt in the boy's pocket.

'He went after a golf-ball,' he told her. He showed it to her. 'Why would he do that?'

The woman pushed straggling hair back into a nest of curlers. She regarded the stinking, wet figure of Root. He didn't meet with her approval.

'Well, 'e wanted to play. 'E had this golf-stick, like. 'E'd seen it on telly. And 'e 'adn't a ball.'

For once Mabbatt had nothing to say.

He turned from the woman.

'I want him within an hour.'

The woman took no notice:

'Willie! Willie! You'll get no tea tonight! It were chips and you won't 'ave 'em.'

'About this golf-stick,' Mabbatt said to her in an unaccustomedly quiet voice. 'I'd like to see it. Please.'

The woman looked up at Mabbatt.

'What for?'

He told her.

Thirty-two

'In a . . . match, if a partner be absent for reasons satisfactory to the Committee, the remaining member(s) of his side may represent the side.'

Root selected a wedge for his shot to the green. He could see that his partner, Jack Lecky, was apprehensive, but Root had no doubts about pitching this one up. With some shots you knew. You could look at the ball, glance at the pin, feel the wind on your face and swing immediately in full confidence that you would put the ball by the pin.

He swung.

The ball rose.

'Great shot!' murmured Frank Bell generously.

'Fair, Arthur,' Strapp allowed himself.

'Always pin high,' said Lecky. 'A beauty.'

'I reckon that's the game,' said Root.

They were about ninety yards from the eighteenth, and the match had been one of those struggles that every golfer loves. There were the glorious shots and the unaccountable disasters. First Lecky and Root would hit one so badly the hole was lost before they left the tee; and then either Strapp or Frank Bell would make a hash of the next hole.

Strapp played well for a man who had taken only six lessons. He pulled off a respectable par four at the difficult eighth, when all that the others could achieve was a five – that was Root – with a lost ball for Frank Bell, and a six for Lecky. But on the eighteenth Root's steadiness prevailed. Frank Bell hit a superb drive which went screaming down the course for over two hundred and sixty yards, to finish in a deep divot scrape and make his shot to the green sheer hell. And he put it into one of the approach bunkers. Strapp took an air shot at the tee, and followed it with a shot that succeeded only in toppling the ball from the plastic peg; with his third he hammered the ball solidly into a thick patch of gorse some fifty yards away. The ball-scrounger, Williamson, marked it down for his evening's glass of beer.

Root watched the exhibition with some amusement.

He and Lecky had come to the eighteenth tee with the match all square. There was everything to play for: twenty pence a corner, Strapp's first game at the club, and Lecky's first round since Elaine's death. Root and Lecky had both driven steadily down the fairway. Jack Lecky's second was well short of the green, and his third a hook out of bounds where the practice-ground adjoined the fairway. So, with Frank in the bunker for two, Root himself a distance of ninety or so yards from the green also for two, and the others out of the match, Root knew that everything depended on his third.

It was a match-winner.

Frank tried hard to bring off an explosion shot, but was still in the bunker when playing his fourth. He hit it hard and it trickled to the edge of the green. Then his putt raced clean across the green.

With five shots played to Root's three, he conceded handsomely.

'Yours!' he called to Root. 'Well played both!'

They shook hands and decided to go for a drink on the terrace.

A ring on the handbell brought Bliss out, his rat's face arranged in a smile. This was his last week at Wolvers. Wisely he had accepted the compensation offered for the loss of his job.

'Four pints, steward,' said Root.

'Yes, sir.'

Lecky muttered under his breath. He couldn't stand the obsequious Bliss.

It was Frank Bell who brought up the subject that they had all managed to hold back for the past three hours.

'What happened to Williamson?'

Strapp shrugged.

'Nothing. He wasn't really withholding information, not in the legal sense. There'd be no point in charging him. He saw the lad, but he didn't think he counted.'

Lecky could accept the macabre irony of it all, but the bitterness persisted. However, he said nothing. He had to learn to live with it. But if Williamson had only said that the mongol was on the course that morning! As it was, he had kept silent and left a deadly situation which could so easily have been resolved.

'If he'd said something!' Frank protested. 'Just a word – if he'd just mentioned the lad was on the course!'

'Yes,' said Arthur Root warningly, with a glance at Jack Lecky.

'And no one else noticed him,' said Strapp. 'It's marvellous. He picked up the one thing that would make him completely acceptable on a golf course. The wedge. The killer's wedge.'

That was how it was, thought Root. The boy, grinning at the excitement of the unfamiliar scene on the busy course, had been shocked out of his inane, gentle, idiot's happiness. Noise burst about him. People rushed towards where he stood beside the spinney in his red anorak that looked so uncannily like Purseglove's at first sight, but on inspection proved to be cheap and frayed.

And he had moved towards the glittering, bloodstained wedge, attracted by the brightness of the steel shaft. Into the spinney. One hand in the undergrowth to collect the club. Then quietly through the brush that was empty of people, for they had all by now congregated beside the corpse of Tom Tyzack. But why, thought Root, had he completed Purseglove's alibi so perfectly? What had impelled him to take off the anorak as he came out of the spinney? Some freak of the idiot's mind?

He walked out of the spinney and across the first fairway. If anyone had seen him – and it was possible, but no one recalled having done so – he was another golfer. He could be seen and not seen. And then he had merged into the bushes and trees.

They sat back in the comfortable cane chairs. Lecky held back his deep sadness by going over the game. Frank Bell's thoughts were of Margaret and Portugal. Strapp, conscious of having held up his end well throughout the match, was wondering just how he had managed to play so badly at the eighteenth. Root was admiring the shaven grass before him. The eighteenth had the best green on the course – level, wide and drained perfectly. You could go for the hole in the knowledge that no contour would glide your ball off-line; and there would be no odd variation of pace, for the grass was even. For the first time he felt a glimmer of pity for the murderer. Purseglove would never play golf again. No club would have him when he came out of gaol; and he would be a broken old man.

They had arrested him at his home. He hadn't tried to run. Root could well imagine the scene. The neat, detached house with Athena reproductions, banks of flowers in full bloom, a copper kettle above the fake coal fire, the once-good furniture covered in pleasant cheap fabrics: the desire to appear comfortably-placed whilst underneath there was the growing realization that there would never be enough money. No one at the club had suspected that Purseglove was such a lowly figure at the Tax Office. And he had no chance whatsoever of making senior grade. The new recruits were qualified men and Purseglove wasn't. It was as simple as that. Purseglove, knowing the secrets of other men's incomes, had felt the bitterness of progressive poverty.

Into the genteel suburb came the police Jaguars; and then Mabbatt. The hoses played into the ground as men stopped cleaning their cars; ladies peered from upper windows to see what the Pursegloves had been up to. Strapp described it later to Root:

214

'I had to keep telling myself he'd pushed a harmless woman off the roof, or I'd have apologized for bothering him. As soon as Mabbatt told him the boy had come round he said it was ridiculous to suggest other than an accident – the boy slipped and he was afraid, so he ran off home. Mabbatt waited for a minute and said he was arresting him for killing Tyzack.'

Root finished his beer.

'More ?' asked Frank Bell.

'Why not ?' said Arthur Root.

The trouble with Purseglove, thought Root, was that he possessed intelligence without astuteness. Like so many others, he had tried to turn his inside knowledge into gain. Mabbatt had seized on the point at once. 'Compared to Tyzack,' the Superintendent had told him, 'you're an amateur. He did you, Purseglove. He liked it, too. I'll bet he laughed like a drain about you !' And Mabbatt sketched in a picture of Purseglove using his knowledge and his intelligence to ferret out the information that would make Tom Tyzack richer and allow Purseglove the furniture and the car and the holiday that were the symbols of success on the neat estate.

Purseglove had been capable enough. He knew the jargon of the departments concerned, and he could easily pass himself off as a qualified enquirer. Tom Tyzack knew what land to buy. And when the time came for the promised payment, he had told Purseglove his treachery would bring no reward. Succinctly and vulgarly, in his mocking, scornful way he had refused to pay the desperate man. Mabbatt even guessed at the words Tom would use. And he would know, thought Root. Mabbatt would enjoy telling Purseglove what kind of treacherous fool he had been.

Purseglove didn't say anything to Mabbatt. Quite composed, he listened to all Mabbatt told him, a dapper figure of great respectability.

Root began his second pint of beer and listened to the desultory conversation of the three men with him.

Strapp saw that Root was quiet.

'Thinking about Purseglove?'

'Aye.'

He looked at Lecky.

For a while, after the revelation that it was his own words that had condemned Elaine Bliss, it had seemed that Lecky might need psychiatric help. As soon as he heard of Purseglove's arrest, he collapsed. And though he looked well enough in the dying sunlight, he still had that sadness about the eyes. He would, thought Root, go over that scene at the bar again and again, each day until he died. One chance remark!

But how could Purseglove have brought himself to kill a woman he had been intimate with? How *could* he! Root shook his head. How *could* Purseglove bring himself to batter Elaine Bliss until, unresisting, she was thrown to her death? Tom Tyzack's murder was almost excusable by comparison!

Root hadn't seen Purseglove except briefly in court. It was enough. He hadn't wanted any memories of that haggard face. Like Lecky, he wanted to forget the whole ghastly, violent business. Yet, sitting here, afterwards, memory would persist. Root could remember almost every word of Strapp's account of his interrogation. Purseglove had not retained his composure for long.

Thirty-three

'An amateur golfer is one who plays the game solely as a non-remunerative or non-profit-making sport.'

'Mabbatt left him alone for an hour or two at the station. I didn't think he was going to crack, but it did the trick. Surprised me, really. But I suppose he'd never seen the inside of a cell before. Mabbatt's a cunning bird,' Strapp told him. 'He wouldn't stop talking. Oh, Mabbatt was happy, all right. Purseglove was chattering away like a lad caught stealing! Mabbatt didn't mention the Bliss woman – Purseglove brought it up himself. He said "I had to push her". *Push* her! That's what he called it – I don't think he ever admitted to himself that he murdered her. Mabbatt just let him go on. He said he'd had to do it because she'd seen enough to give him away. He'd convinced himself as soon as he heard it that it was the only thing he could do – kill her to shut her up. It was at the Dance. All she said was "You lost your ball in the woods". She'd heard it from Lecky. She was only trying to make conversation – that was the sort of woman she was. Ah, but you'd know that,' Strapp said. 'He understood her to mean that she'd actually seen him go off into the woods during the Irish match. If she started saying she'd seen him lose his ball or go after it, there'd be talk – someone would soon be asking how he came to win if he'd been off the fairway! So he thought she'd seen whoever it was that had given him his alibi. The mongol lad, as we know now. He still hadn't a clue who it was – he was worked up about it all that week, trying to think who it could be!

He had known about Jack Lecky and Elaine Bliss, thought Root. Very clever about personal relationships, was Des Purseglove. He'd known by the way Elaine behaved that she had begun a new affair. He got quite agitated about it. He said to Mabbatt: "I knew you'd find him, but I couldn't! There's only one of me! Where could I start looking! Where! I'm not the police! I'm not a professional!" '

'He hadn't wanted to hurt either of them, he said – wished them the best of luck and all that. When they went up to the tower he followed. Oh, he knew he'd been lucky! He went up the back stairs behind the Great Hall. And no one saw him! When he got to the top, he cracked Lecky's head against the stonework and didn't give Mrs Bliss any time to talk.'

And that had been that, thought Root.

Evidence had been forthcoming almost immediately. Purseglove's dinner-suit bore traces of blood and hair, Lecky's blood, Elaine's hair: a diary with Ministry phone-numbers; Mrs Church's statement, which, checked carefully, revealed a hurried Purseglove arriving via the ladies' entrance. The collapse of Purseglove's alibi; the residual traces of blood and hair on the head of the pitching-wedge: they were more than enough to gain a conviction.

Root was well down his second pint of beer. The others were talking, sometimes about the game, sometimes about the murder of Tom Tyzack. Jack Lecky didn't seem too bad. Root didn't join in much. He wanted to organize his thoughts. Root was not an intellectual. He found difficulty in understanding the processes that led him to take decisions; even less how he came to an acceptance of the brutal and violent cases he had been involved in.

218

He knew, however, that there would be a time when he could look back on the double killing and point to a *reason* for the murders : say to himself 'Aye, Tom said *this*' or 'Tom did *that*'; and there would be a calmness in his mind again.

It mattered very much that it should happen.

Root looked down the eighteenth. There was a halt in the conversation.

'What do you think, Arthur ?' asked Frank Bell.

He recalled the thread of the conversation. It had centred on Tom Tyzack's character.

The moment came.

'Tom was always joking.'

They waited for him to go on, recognizing that he had been abstracted and was now gathering his thoughts.

'Tom,' said Root. 'Tom was the sort of person that never got further than the school playground – I don't reckon he was ever an adult. He never grew up ! It was like having an adolescent around, someone say thirteen or fourteen. Big and awkward. Bigger than the others.' His thoughts were clearer now. 'He was a cruel bastard.'

Tom had often played practical jokes on people he disliked: sometimes the results had been hilarious.

He went on :

'He'd be a cruel bastard if you crossed him, and he'd laugh himself sick if someone came to a sticky end. That was Tom's trouble – I don't think he ever gave a thought to what might come after a joke. He didn't *have* to tell Purseglove about Jenny Piggott and the maggot farm !' He was digressing, but Strapp, Jack and Frank understood. Or they seemed to. 'He could have kept it to himself ! And he could have done something to keep Des happy – I mean, what would a few hundred have been to Tom ? He could have given him something on account – promised him more. Just to let Des Purseglove keep his self-respect ! But Tom wasn't that sort ! He had to make him look a complete noddy ! That's adolescent behaviour. Lads that age never show mercy ! Not Tom's type. If there's another kid in the bunch who's handicapped – if he stutters or if he's a bit spastic, they never let up. With Tom it was money. If he saw that someone was jealous

219

of him, he never let them forget what he was. He loved it, all of it – the big car, the women, the property deals, flying off to the Canaries when he felt like a break. I know a dozen men in the club who hated him for it. Just for that. Showing that he could do just as he liked, because he was Tom Tyzack!'

The others waited again for him to go on.

He looked into the bottom of his glass. It was late. He'd have to go home soon. Tonight he was back on the beat. With luck, the brick-thief would reveal himself. If not, there was another night, another week. He found himself talking again, quite vehemently: 'Did he have to tell Purseglove he'd left the girl the maggot farm!'

What a twist of the knife that must have been for genteelly-impoverished Purseglove, whose wife had confided to their neighbours that they were going to take their annual holiday in Greece! How it must have curdled inside him as the secret jibes accompanied the play on that Sunday morning! Root could picture Purseglove's final moment of agony: according to Purseglove's story, Tyzack had spotted the golf-ball they were searching for. Before he called out that he had the ball, Purseglove came up to him. Purseglove couldn't believe that he was to get no money. He had followed Tyzack into the spinney to ask again. He wasn't searching for Frank's golf-ball – he hadn't troubled to bring a golf-club with him. The sight of that earnest, intent taxman's face drove Tyzack to paroxysms of subdued laughter; he laughed so much that he didn't – or couldn't – call out that he had found the golf-ball. And he had reinforced the joke.

In the damp spinney, with its quiet searchers, its cautious thrushes, its dripping bushes and sparkling leaves, Tyzack had come to the cream of his sustained joke.

Purseglove's recounting of the story had impressed Strapp. 'You could see,' he had told Root, 'that he still doesn't believe it – he's still in a daze, or he was when he told the tale to Mabbatt. There was this emptiness in his eyes – the bottom of his world had fallen out!'

Tyzack had told him that he had willed the maggot farm away. His words had been a coarse jest:

'When the worms get me, she'll get maggots! and you'll get bugger all!'

Purseglove had misunderstood. He took it to mean that Jenny had already been given the farm.

What followed had a terrible inevitability.

Tom ferreted into a tangle of brambles and long grass with his pitching-wedge. Purseglove watched Tyzack's bull-neck; he was shaking with grief, whilst Tyzack chuckled quietly.

But Tom shouldn't have picked the ball up!

Of course it couldn't have been played, not from where it lay. Frank would have had to drop out behind the spinney, declaring his ball unplayable. Maybe Tyzack had assumed that Frank would do so; had he meant to give Frank the ball? Tom wasn't known as a golf-cheat. Perhaps he had picked the ball up, meaning to hand it to Frank? It would save time. But Frank should have been told where his ball lay and given an opportunity to decide what to do!

Why *had* he picked up the ball?

Perhaps he had been so preoccupied with the thought of Purseglove's ridiculously shocked, hating face that he had forgotten about the ownership of the golf-ball?

Had he meant to cheat?

Had he meant to steal the ball because of its value as an invention?

Probably not, decided Root. Parsons was right about Tom. Tom had been a man. Not a cheat; not at golf, anyway.

He had paid for his contempt of Purseglove.

As he parted the grass and brambles with two hands, Tyzack made the only serious miscalculation of his life. He handed his pitching-wedge to Purseglove.

'Hold this bugger,' he chuckled.

He reached for the ball and slipped it into his pocket. And he was still shaking with silent laughter.

Purseglove struck. Struck and struck again. Threw the club to the edge of the spinney. Panicked. Controlled himself and slipped out of the spinney. Took a cigarette from his bag.

Well, thought Root, it's all over. Three familiar faces gone from Wolvers. He decided against a third pint. There was night duty to think of. And yet another letter about the expenses he had not yet received.

Frank Bell could be philosophical about the whole unpleasant business. His invention had been assessed; an offer would be forthcoming. He need not imagine, the manufacturers told him, that he would make a fortune. He interrupted Root's thoughts:

'So Tom's last joke killed him?'

'It did,' agreed Strapp, who was still puzzled about the arc of his backswing. Slow, yes. Low, yes. He could understand that. But what about the moment when you changed from a backswing to a forward motion? He was immediately excited. Could it be that he had been making the elementary error of swaying? 'Yes, it killed him,' he said.

Lecky got up.

'It killed Elaine too.'

Thirty-four

'. . . a player is not permitted to play in two ways and then choose his score.'

A week after Purseglove was sentenced to life imprisonment, Mabbatt was at home pasting a memento of the Tyzack case on to the living-room wall. It looked well. Jenny would approve.

The figures on the map looked back at him. The foursome doddering towards the first green: that clever bloody PC who had kept his eyes open; neat Elaine Bliss neatly ringed in black; lecherous Parsons; Bliss at his bright blue tent, obsequious, rat-faced and sly; Williamson, the stupid bastard who had nearly done him down over the case. And all the rest. But he had brought it off. With Blore in poor shape, there would be a change of Chief Superintendent soon. Jenny would show her appreciation.

Mabbatt stood back from the wall.

There was something missing.

He drank a bottle of beer without troubling to find a glass. Then he went for a black felt pen.

It took him a few minutes to get it right. It wasn't really true any more. But it was the right idea.

When he had finished, an inexpertly-pencilled gallows stood beside the spinney. Dangling freely was Purseglove.

Mabbatt smiled.

At six on the same day, Jack Lecky returned to his semi-detached house.

It was emptier than ever. He turned the telly on and then remembered that he had not yet fixed the aerial. Black and white shadows danced zanily across the screen. Tomorrow, he thought, I'll do it then.

At five-thirty next morning, Arthur Root smiled beatifically. He was standing in a workman's shelter beside a building-site. And he was looking at the invisible brick-thief's transport. He had seen it a hundred times before: seen it and seen it, just like the killer on the golf course.

Silent. Powerful. And leaving no tracks. None that shouldn't have been there. It delivered at the site every morning at this time. Root waited. Soon, the milkman would come from behind the pile of bricks behind the houses.